THE BALLAD OF ELMO BOGG

C.F. LEWIS

CHAPTER 1

The rusted El Camino cruised down the highway like poop through a goose. The two scrawny men inside wore dark shades and said little as they jammed to a tune from long ago. The air conditioner worked, but not very well, so the extra-large blue Slurpee they each sipped on helped some with the heat.

Elmo Bogg and Melvin Perkins were poverty-stricken and hell-bound. They had both just been fired from Delbert's Grocery. Bagging groceries wasn't a great gig, but it was all they had been able to find. The men had sticky fingers and massive numbers of candy bars kept disappearing each time the men were at work. When the manager walked by the back of their El Camino and noticed a graveyard of candy bar wrappers, the jig was up. When they were not stealing, the boys were getting in confrontations with customers or taking hour-long bathroom breaks. The manager had had enough and relieved them of their gainful employment. This turn of events left the boys in a nastier mood than usual as they cruised.

Jerry Henry was taking his weekly jog up Lakeside Road, and he was at peace with the world around him. It had been a long time since Jerry had felt peace. He had loved his wife and his best friend very much, but his wife and best friend had ended up loving each other very much. It had been a year of pain and sorrow, but he was fighting to emerge from the black hole of despair. The birds were singing again, and the sun was shining again. Having put on a little too much weight over the winter, he had faithfully committed to a weekly five-mile jog each Saturday. Somehow the jogging was therapy for the broken heart and for all the built-up tension of the looming court battle with his wife. He could not help but smile as he soaked in the beautiful day. He would not be smiling much longer.

Elmo and Melvin spotted him at a distance and made the decision without saying a word.

"Melvin, how much Slurpee you got left?"

"About half a cup, I'd say, Elmo. You feeling it today?"

"Oh, I'm feeling it all right. Pour the rest of yours into my cup and be ready to take the wheel," said Elmo with a wicked smile spreading across his face. "This boy is about to have a bad day."

Elmo gunned the El Camino and as it came up beside Jerry Henry, Melvin grabbed the wheel and held it steady from the passenger seat. Elmo carefully leaned out the window as far as he could with the blue Slurpee. Jerry had his earphones on and was jamming out to something with a lively beat, so he did not hear a thing as Elmo slammed 64 ounces of blue-dyed sugar all across the front of his chest and face.

All he saw was blue swallowing him up as he wiped out on the side of the road. The pavement scratched him from here to yonder as he went head over heels in a terrible collision with the ground. As he ripped the headphones off and stood back up on shaky legs, he was in shock and disbelief. His white shirt and shorts were now blue. His arms and face were blue to match. His entire body hurt. The revelation of what had just happened slowly became clear to Jerry as the El Camino slammed on its brakes about a hundred feet away. Elmo and Melvin hopped out of their vehicle and were bent over, laughing hysterically.

"Look, Melvin," shouted Elmo, barely able to breathe, laugh, and talk at the same time. "It's Fat Ass Smurf! What's the matter, old boy? You looked thirsty. You owe me a dollar and twenty-five cents!"

"Papa Smurf needs you back home, boy! You need a lift? Are you sad? Are you feeling blue?" shouted Melvin as he and Elmo danced around and celebrated the most excellent bombing raid.

A rage began to flow over and through Jerry that he had never known before. He began to shake from head to toe, and his eyes glazed over. He began to beat his chest and screamed out a murderous, soul-wrenching scream toward the heavens. The terrible howl was so scary, Elmo and Melvin took it as their cue to jump in the El Camino and haul butt down the road before Jerry could get a hold of them as he was a very large and muscular individual. As they laughed and giggled about their bombing raid, Jerry was soon a small blip in their rearview mirror. The country was very flat so they could still see him as they were about to disappear over the horizon. The cruel and evil act made them somehow feel better about their own problems. Very suddenly, their back left tire blew out with a sound as loud as a shotgun blast. They quickly stopped laughing as they pulled to the side of the road.

Jerry Henry stopped screaming at the sky as he heard the unmistakable boom of the blow out. Jerry started to run like a great locomotive toward the horizon where he could still make out the now very small image of the El Camino far in the distance. He ran like there was a great and powerful engine hidden somewhere deep within him. He poured all the pain of the divorce and betrayal into his legs as they blurred down the road. A nasty grin spread across Jerry's blue face as he chased his vengeance.

Elmo was overseeing Melvin as he put the jack under their vehicle and was trying to get the old, rusted relic to actually work. "You better hurry up with that jack, Melvin. That blue bastard is really soaking up ground. He was a big dude, and he's looking bigger by the second."

"I'm trying my best, Elmo, but this jack is worthless," replied Melvin.

Jerry was moving like an unstoppable force now, and he looked bigger and bigger as he got closer and closer. Elmo was now entering the realm of panic as he cheered Melvin on. Melvin now had the vehicle jacked up and was starting to spin lug nuts off. Jerry was screaming as he ran, and the screaming was getting louder and louder as the blue train got ever closer. Elmo and Melvin were never going to be invited to fight in the octagon; scrawny was an understatement—both men's weight combined did not weigh what one of Jerry's legs weighed. Jerry was now within two hundred feet of the El Camino and closing in on his target very quickly. He looked like a man possessed with eyes bulging!

"Abandon ship, abandon ship!" screamed Elmo as he abandoned the El Camino and began running as fast as his bony legs could carry him. Melvin had joined in the mad retreat as they tried to put distance between themselves and Jerry, but it was no use. Jerry first swallowed up

Elmo and began to beat him like a madman. He punched and kicked the writhing Elmo, and then ripped off Elmo's belt and began to beat him like an insane conductor in the devil's orchestra. Elmo was trying to slither away like a handicapped snake, but it was no use. Jerry was surgical with that belt. Little Melvin, always faithful to his buddy, ran back and tried to help, but ended up getting his own backside lit up like it was the fourth of July.

When Jerry's arm was too tired to swing the belt anymore, he took a deep breath, realized he felt somewhat better about life, and continued on his jog. Elmo and Melvin dragged themselves back to the El Camino and headed back to their old shack where they treated each other's wounds the best they could. Both of their rumps were covered in red welts. It was a week before either man could sit down without crying. It would be years before either man would choose blue at the Slurpee machine again without PTSD filling their little black hearts.

CHAPTER 2

It seemed as though both God and the devil had been trying to stomp on Elmo Bogg his entire life, but he kept scurrying around like a little roach that just refused to die. Elmo lived in a small town called Eltonberry in the heartland of America. Some people in town referred to Elmo as an outlaw, but all the people in town referred to Elmo as an outcast. Elmo grew up on the wrong side of the tracks as poor as a person could be and still survive. His mother was a promiscuous drug addict that could never quite seem to pull her act together. She loved Elmo, but she was never much on mothering. Elmo ended up raising himself for the most part.

Elmo's only true friend was another outcast named Melvin Perkins. Elmo and Melvin had met in elementary school. The two boys seemed to understand from an early age that they were basically alone in a world that did not care for them very much, so they decided to take care of each other the best they could. They became inseparable through the years. Elmo and Melvin spent most of their nine years of high school being stuffed in lockers, given wedgies, and mistreated in a variety of ways by the athletes at their school. When the athletes got bored with them, the two boys made history by getting picked on by the Beta Club, Math Club, Chess Club, and even the Young Christian Soldier Club. The boys became true legends when even the lunch ladies started stuffing them in cafeteria freezers.

Now, Elmo may have been mistreated all his life, but he never took it lying down. He was a game bird and always ready for a fight. The only problem being, he was more than just a little scrawny and always ended up taking a beating to some degree or another. Elmo loved the concept of keeping score. He even made his sidekick Melvin carry around a little black book to keep a running count on how much vengeance and payback he owed his tormentors.

Fast forward another twelve years, and things were not a whole lot different. Life still seemed to be violating the two men at every possible opportunity. Elmo and Melvin shared a little two-bedroom shack on the edge of town. It was not much, but it was all they could afford on the measly income they brought home. Both men bounced from one minimum-wage job to another, and neither man seemed to be capable of keeping any job for long. When they could not find regular work, they collected scrap metal in the back of the El Camino. Working as a team, they usually made enough to keep a little gas in the El Camino, stay just ahead of eviction, and keep Thursday night sacred.

Thursday night was their favorite night of the week. The Greasy Spoon Diner's special on Thursday night was always fried chicken with mashed potatoes and gravy. It was the only real luxury the two men afforded themselves, and they were faithful on the matter. As Elmo pulled up in the parking lot of the diner, he and Melvin immediately noticed the patrol car of Sheriff John Duffie. Duffie was a bully and had been his entire life. Elmo and Melvin hated him with a passion. The feeling was very mutual. Sheriff Duffie looked for every opportunity to make the two men's lives a living hell. He had been doing this since they were all in grade school. It was a running feud, you might say. Being a lawman and huge, it seemed Duffie got the better end of the feud most of the time.

As Elmo walked through the front door, it did not take Sheriff Duffie long to get started. He was sitting with three of his deputies and was hungry for trouble.

"Well, look what the cat dragged in, boys! It's Tweedle-Dee and Tweedle-Dumbass," said Duffie, as his entire table erupted into laughter.

"Duffie, if I would have known you were going to be here, I'd have brought your mom's panties back. She left them over at the house the other night. Melvin and I used them as a tent when we went camping, her ass being as big as that table you're sitting at. It worked out really well for us. Thank her for us when you see her," said Elmo.

Duffie immediately jumped up and was towering over Elmo. "It's about time you learned the meaning of police brutality, you little squirt."

"Jackie," shouted Elmo to the waitress watching it all go down. "Go get me the two biggest pieces of bread you can find and an entire jar of mayonnaise. I'm about to have the biggest bacon sandwich this town has ever seen," said little Elmo, standing up with his fists clenched and back arched. "It's time for the slaughterhouse, you pig, and I'm the butcher. Say when, Duffie."

"When," shouted Sheriff Duffie as he slapped Elmo a ringing blow across the face which sent him down to the floor so fast his feet went straight up in the air. Duffie was about to continue the beating when he caught sight of Judge Clayton walking in his direction. Judge Clayton was a big man in their county and one of the few that could make Sheriff Duffie behave himself.

"Sheriff, is there a problem here?" asked Judge Clayton in a very menacing tone.

"No, sir, Judge. I was about to haul these two in for assaulting an officer and disturbing the peace. They're troublemakers from start to finish," said Duffie, puffing his chest out.

"Go about your business, Sheriff, and consider yourself lucky that I'm not going to have charges pressed against you for abusing your office," said Judge Clayton as he helped Elmo up.

"Are you all right, son?" asked the Judge.

"Yes, I'm all right. Thanks for your help," replied Elmo. "Jackie, we'll take our two chicken dinners to go tonight, and please put them in paper bags and not plastic."

Out in the parking lot, Elmo and Melvin got into the car and started it up. Elmo was simmering with anger over the confrontation with Duffie.

"Melvin, did you bring the black book tonight?"

"Of course," replied Melvin. "I never go anywhere without it."

"Put another check by Duffie's name. How many does that make for him?"

"Elmo, there must be at least a thousand checks in here for that moron."

"Before we sleep tonight, Melvin, we'll be able to scratch a few of those checks off the list. I smell vengeance in the air."

Elmo punched the accelerator and sped off into the night. A couple of miles outside of town, Elmo pulled the car over on the side of the road and killed the engine. He slowly turned toward Melvin and held up a set of keys, smiling a wicked grin. "Payback time for our fine Sheriff, the great jackass of Eltonberry. He is going to regret this night, I promise you. It's time to reap the whirlwind."

"What do you have in mind, Elmo, and why are we stopped in the middle of nowhere? And whose keys are you holding?" asked Melvin, very confused.

"Just follow me," said Elmo, getting out of the car. Elmo took their chicken dinners out of the paper bags and offered up a menacing laugh to the darkness of the night. Holding the paper bags carefully as if they were a newly found treasure, he headed off into some thick brush on the side of the road with Melvin following close behind. When he was satisfied that no one could see them from the road, Elmo unbuckled his pants, pulled them down to his ankles, and squatted over one of the paper bags. As Elmo grunted and strained, Melvin was in complete shock at what was taking place in front of him.

"What, in the name of all that is holy, are you doing? That slap back at the diner must have jarred something loose in your head!" Melvin Perkins had been raised by a crazy mother, and, as a result, he would lose control of his nerves whenever he was in the presence of anything he deemed crazy. His hands would begin to shake, and his left leg would always bounce. He was shaking and bouncing all over the place as he stared in disbelief at the bizarre image of Elmo pooping in the paper bag his chicken dinner had been resting comfortably in not five minutes earlier.

"Melvin, get busy filling your bag up, I'll explain in a few minutes," said Elmo, grunting with the work at hand.

"You've got to be kidding me. There's no way I can do this, nor do I want to do it," said Melvin, disgusted.

"Melvin, I don't need excuses!" shouted Elmo. "I need turds, and I need them in that paper bag, now. Are you my right-hand man or not?"

Melvin took a deep breath, and then begrudgingly did the dastardly deed. Ten minutes later, they were back on the road, their packages in the back of the El Camino. They pulled up to a nice two-story home at the end of a long driveway. It was a beautiful home and belonged to Sheriff John Duffie. The Sheriff was working the graveyard shift and shouldn't be home before morning. Elmo and Melvin hid their car in the shadows, grabbed their special bags, and walked right up to the front door.

"When that big bastard got up in my face at the diner, I took the liberty of liberating his keys from his belt." Elmo figured correctly that Duffie was too arrogant to think he would need any alarm system, him being sheriff. Elmo tried keys until he found one that opened the front door. The two men wasted no time. They went straight upstairs and found Duffie's bedroom. Elmo had brought a small bag of tools in; he used a pry bar to very carefully pull back a sheet of the wood paneling that covered Duffie's bedroom walls.

A man that had never smelled an aging turd in a paper bag had no idea just how brutal a smell it was. It was an unforgiving smell that wrapped itself around the very soul of a man, and it did not get better with time. "If we hide these bags really good, the smell will slowly drive that jackass crazy. He'll never think to look in the paneling, and even if he did, he would have to tear half this house apart to pinpoint where the smell is actually coming from once it starts spreading," whispered Elmo.

They wedged the bags behind insulation and wiring in such a way that it was almost invisible, even when you were looking directly at it. They carefully put the paneling back, and, before leaving, they turned the thermostat up a couple of degrees to make sure it was nice and warm when Duffie got home. Like phantoms in the night, the two men were gone just as quietly as they had come in.

As they drove home, both men had a very contented and peaceful feeling. They had gained a little bit of ground in this great war of attrition.

"Melvin, you can erase two or three check marks under that pig's name."

"Elmo, I'm a little worried how you know so much about the smell of aging turds in paper bags. Do I really want to know the history on that?"

"No, Melvin, you do not. You really don't."

Neither man said anything else as they got home, enjoyed their cold chicken dinners, and prepared for bed. After watching some television, they each simply went to their bedrooms, fell asleep, and dreamed of the look on Duffie's face as he frantically tried to understand the terrible smell invading his world. Just before morning, Elmo dreamed of a treasure chest. Just before he was able to open it, he bolted upright in his bed. He took it as a sign that it was time to get serious about making his fortune and finding some meaning in his life.

CHAPTER 3

When Sheriff Duffie got home from working the graveyard shift, he was truly exhausted. He wanted to go inside, take a shower, and sleep for just as long as he possibly could. He had to take his hideaway key out of a plastic raccoon he kept beside his front steps, because his keys had mysteriously disappeared while he was at work the previous night. He spent a solid two hours tearing through both his police cruiser and his office to no avail. He wasn't too distraught since he always kept spare keys around, but still, one never enjoyed the feeling of helplessness that accompanied the losing of one's keys.

It was not until he got into his upstairs master bedroom that he realized something was very wrong. A nasty odor was covering the room in an awful manner. It smelled very much like sewage to him. He went into the master bathroom and began to study the toilet. To his surprise, the toilet looked fine, and the smell was not stronger near the toilet. Wax seal might be bad on the toilet, he figured, but he did not have the energy to pursue the matter at the moment. He showered and laid down on his bed. If he could just rest his eyes for a few moments, everything would be okay. But there was just no way—the smell was still there and seemed to be growing worse with each passing second. Lying on the bed, he tried to doze off, but his nose was actually burning. The smell was brutal.

He finally could not take it anymore and went to the guest bedroom downstairs. After his nap, he would call the plumber to come pump out his tank, change the wax seal, and just do whatever it took to deal with the smell. The plumber came and did his thing, but he was at a loss and could find nothing wrong. He presented the Sheriff with a large bill and left. The smell did not leave.

Over the next several weeks, every third day or so, Elmo and Melvin would make more bombing raids on the Sheriff's house. The boys would hide their terrible turd bags in impossible to find places all over the house. They even hit the kitchen and dining room. There would be no escape. The smell was like an invading Mongolian Army, swallowing up everything in its path.

Duffie was at his wit's end. He felt like he was going crazy. The smell was destroying his life. His girlfriend was not returning his calls, people were avoiding getting near him at work, and he had spent over eight hundred dollars on multiple plumbers and cleaning ladies. On a whim, he even had the local Catholic priest come over and sprinkle holy water throughout the entire house in case there were evil spirits behind the vile smell. A girl scout knocked on his door trying to sell cookies. When he opened the door, she made a terrible face and just ran away. Even the Jehovah's Witnesses were leaving him alone.

CHAPTER 4

M elvin arrived back at the shack about ten o'clock in the morning. He had made an early trip into town to pick up a few groceries. "Elmo, you said to get back over here in a hurry. What is the big rush? Are we gonna take care of some names in the black book today?"

"No, we are not, Melvin. We are heading in the exact opposite direction, as a matter of fact. It is time for us to get serious about making our fortune. Collecting scrap metal and stocking groceries is not going to get us there. I saw a program on the television last night about a preacher that was going off to Africa to help some kids or some such thing, but he was flying out on his own private jet. It occurred to me that if a fellow must work, he might as well work for the richest man in town. Who is richer than the Almighty God, Melvin?"

"I don't know, Elmo."

"The answer is nobody, Melvin. It can't be too hard to be a preacher. Talk about the Lord, eat fried chicken, and wear lots of hair spray. We will be on our own private jet in no time. We might even get to comfort some good-looking widow women in our spare time."

"Are we also going to help any children in Africa?" asked Melvin, excited at the thought of doing something good in life.

"My God, Melvin, can you stay focused for five minutes, please? Jets, widows, and lots of money has got to be our focus right now. If it works out that we can help some snot-nosed kids along the way, I am not opposed to that. Just keep your priorities straight, we are trying to make our fortune here."

"Elmo, I'm not sure, but I imagine that a preacher has got to have some license or paperwork before the local pastor is going to let him get behind his pulpit."

"Poor, stupid Melvin, I'm always two steps ahead of you, son. I have already thought this out. We're going to start with the black church on Dublin Street. It's one of the smaller churches in town. You gotta crawl before you walk. Elder Johnson at the Church of Transformation is going to welcome me with open arms this Sunday morning, and he just doesn't know it, yet."

"How are you going to pull that off?"

"I'm not, Melvin, you are. I want you to call up Elder Johnson this afternoon and pretend to be from the NAACP. Tell Elder Johnson that I am some great champion of civil rights, blah, blah, blah. Tell him I am passing through this way, and I feel the Lord leading me to minister to the flock located where my humble beginning was. Just talk me up and tell him that signs and miracles will follow. He will sop that up like tomato gravy."

For the rest of the day, Elmo and Melvin made their plans and spent money they didn't have. Just before dark, Melvin placed a call to Elder Johnson and laid it on thick.

Much to Melvin's surprise, it worked. Elder Johnson hung up the phone with a big spiritual hook in his mouth.

"Some people would be pretty nervous speaking in front of a crowd. Do you really think you can pull this off, Elmo?"

"Hell yes, I was born for this kind of stuff, and I've got lots of plans for my first service. If I can become a legend at the beginning of my ministry, the churches will line up to hear me speak from now on. I have been studying all kinds of religions on the computer down at the library. I can already see those offering plates full and overflowing. They'll be throwing money at us before this is over."

"Have you ever actually said a real prayer, Elmo, or talked to God or anything of the sort?"

"Quit sweating the small stuff, Melvin. You worry too much. Does your cousin over in Oakdale still work at that reptile farm where they study the snakes? We're going to need him to do us a small favor."

CHAPTER 5

When Sunday morning rolled around, Elmo and Melvin took a taxi to the Church of Transformation. They didn't think the rusted El Camino gave off the right vibe for a great minister. Elmo made Melvin get out of the taxi one block away so he could walk up to the church. Melvin didn't like walking anywhere, but he reluctantly agreed and started walking for the rear of the church. Elmo did not want anyone to see him in the company of Melvin or take notice of the large, brown crate that Melvin would be sneaking in the back door of the church. Elder Johnson's congregation ran about sixty-five members each Sunday morning, and he always stood outside the front door and shook each hand as the church members and visitors came through the door. When he saw Elmo, Elder Johnson was a little confused. When Elmo introduced himself as the visiting evangelist, Elder Johnson was even more confused, but he took it in stride. God surely did work in mysterious ways.

This was no laid-back church. The place was jumping as the choir began to sing. Worship and praise were going up, and Elmo could feel himself getting caught up in the Spirit of the whole thing. By the time the service was handed over to him, the place was on fire. Hands were being raised in worship, the sick had been anointed with oil, and a few sisters of the Lord were even dancing a little jig in the aisle. Soon enough, the welcome had been given, the announcements made, and the song service had come to an end. As Elder Johnson handed him the microphone, he felt a little intimidated, but he was ready. It was go time. The devil was screwed. Elmo Bogg was in the house.

"How many of you love the Lord?" shouted Elmo.

Amens and shouts went up in a fury of adoration. This was going to be easier than he thought. The congregation was primed and ready. All he had to do was throw a little gas on the fire. Before he even said a word, Elmo let out a scream like a wild cat with a rocking chair on his tail.

"Who came here to praise Him?" screamed Elmo.

The shouts kept coming, and one or two of the men were even out in the aisle doing a little praise dance. The congregation was really sopping it up. This was it. Elmo Bogg had found his place. The energy in the sanctuary was electric.

"We are going to talk today about a little subject you may have heard of before. It's called racism."

Hands and handkerchiefs were being waved all over the building, and tears were starting to flow.

"We all have influences in our lives, brothers and sisters. My own father was a professed racist and member of a skinhead biker gang."

One dear old sister on the front pew appeared to almost faint under Elmo's heavy words, but someone seemed to catch her just before she fell. "My father," said Elmo, "never once called me by my Christian name. That's right, folks. My old man referred to me by one of two names for the entire eight months I knew him. Those two names were dumbass and Cinderella. He was determined to turn me into a hater like himself, but there was another influence in my life, dear friends. I would say most of you do not remember me, but I am the son of Wilma Bogg from Davelle Street right here in Eltonberry. God rest her sainted soul."

At the mention of his mother, Elmo thought he noticed several of the men snap their heads to attention. No doubt, they were reminded of the memories of their own sweet mothers. More handkerchiefs were being waved all over the congregation in anticipation of the upcoming victory Elmo was about to profess.

"My mother taught me something very different. My mother told me on more than one occasion that colored men were more than adequate. Many days, I would get off the school bus to find kindly black men coming out of my mother's front door soaking wet with sweat after having worked on our appliances all day out of the kindness of their own hearts. And my poor mother, laid up in the bed sweating out a terrible fever of her own, so out of breath that she could barely speak. Our appliances broke down a lot; they broke down literally every day for a long time. As I look out across the sanctuary this morning, I see so many of those same sweat-soaked faces in this house of worship today, and on behalf of my mother and myself, we say a heartfelt thank you."

The handkerchiefs had stopped waving, and a terrible hush had fallen over the crowd. Most every man in the building had his head bowed and his eyes closed. All the women in the building knew all too well the terrible rumors surrounding Wilma Bogg of Davelle Street. Several wives were just staring at their men in a strange and menacing way. Elder Johnson seemed to be in shock and not sure what to do. The story of Elmo's mother seemed to really touch a nerve with the congregation. Elmo was amazed that his own silver tongue could bring a hush over such a crowd. The place was so quiet, you could have heard a mouse fart anywhere in the building. Elmo then proceeded to name many of those kindly men from so long ago. Many of the men burst into tears as Elmo called their name in thanks for all that sweat and hard work of years gone by. Take that, devil. Elmo Bogg was definitely in the house!

"Now, who is ready for a miracle?" shouted Elmo.

One old sister began to squeal like a mountain lion, and the rest of the church started getting warmed up again. Elmo closed his eyes as if he were walking through dark places in his spirit.

"There is someone here under the sound of my voice that has recently had an accident, a life-changing accident. You know who you are, now come on up here."

Just at that moment and right on cue, Melvin stood up and made his way to the front of the church. Per Elmo's directions, Melvin had hidden one of his arms inside his sweater. Now, the church was a little suspicious that the miracle would involve the only other white man in the building, but they tried to give the benefit of the doubt.

"Come on up here, son. What is your name, young man?"

"My name is Melvin, preacher."

"Have you ever met me before, Melvin?"

"No, sir, I have not," replied Melvin.

"What happened to your arm, Brother Melvin?"

"I lost it to a shark when I was teaching orphans how to swim outside of Galveston, Texas, preacher," replied Melvin, starting to cry.

"Your life is much more difficult now, isn't it, Brother Melvin?"

"I can't even wipe my own behind anymore, preacher. You would think the left hand is adequate, but it's not. I make terrible messes. I have seen hundreds of preachers and doctors, but none of them could help me. It's no use."

"Come here to me, boy. Were any of those doctors or preachers named Elmo Bogg?" shouted Elmo. "I didn't think so. It's go time!"

At just that moment, Elmo laid hands on Melvin's forehead. Melvin went down on cue, and when he stood back up, there were two arms where there had been only one. Elmo thought the place would be going hog wild crazy at that moment, but you could have heard a pin drop. There was no dancing, shouting, praying, or movement at all. It barely looked like folks were breathing. There were just sixty-five very confused and insulted church members staring a silent hole through the middle of the two men in the front of the church. Elmo made the quick decision to bring out the grand finale. If this didn't get them going, nothing would.

No one had noticed the wooden crate that Melvin had snuck in and sat next to the pulpit before the service began. That was about to change.

"How many of you are believers? The bible says you can handle serpents and not be harmed. Kiss our ass, devil! It's go time!"

At that moment, Elmo reached down, opened the crate, and pulled out a six-foot-long boa constrictor that was almost too heavy for him to lift. Melvin reached in and grabbed two smaller handfuls of snakes and threw them out into the congregation. Elmo leaped from the platform into the midst of the church, spinning and dancing in circles with the snake wrapped around him. Elmo began to scream as loud as he could as he danced with the snake. It looked like roaches when the lights come on. People were screaming in terror, clutching their hearts, passing out, and trampling each other as they ran for the exits. Black people obviously did not care for snakes. Melvin was steadily tossing smaller reptiles all over the place. People were so filled with fear, they abandoned their own good senses and their children. Three elders were trampled in the stampede for the exits. Worst of all, a candle was knocked over into some draperies. A blaze was soon burning in a church that had survived for sixty-seven years through tornadoes, termites, floods, and the civil rights movement.

Elmo had got so caught up in his dancing, he had not realized the snake had been slowly tightening up on his neck. As the room went black, Elmo passed out and hit the floor with the snake still wrapped around his neck. Melvin quickly grabbed him by the leg and pulled him from the burning church. Once in the parking lot, Melvin went to work on the snake to make him release his death grip on Elmo's neck. Apparently bored, the snake finally let go and slithered off into the surrounding brush.

The fire department responded quickly, and the little blaze was put out. The church suffered a lot of smoke damage and would need new draperies, new carpet, and a lot of other repairs, but it could have been much worse. Sheriff Duffie was called by Elder Johnson, but he had to explain to the congregation that Elmo could not be arrested for being a horrible human being. As bad as his performance was, he had not actually committed a crime per se. Hating Elmo deeply, Sheriff Duffie tried to convince the church members to lynch Elmo, but they refused after talking it over seriously for a few minutes. Several ladies in the congregation had become overwhelmed and slapped Elmo across the face. Elder Johnson quickly called the ladies down and reprimanded their behavior, but when Elmo demanded to be paid for his preaching that morning, even Elder Johnson slapped Elmo a ringing blow across the face.

CHAPTER 6

E lmo laid in bed and sulked at God and country for a day or two after his great failure at preaching. It occurred to Elmo that if God didn't want his services, maybe the devil was hiring. The more he thought about the prospect, the more excited he began to get. Elmo instructed Melvin to stop by the library and pick up every book he could find pertaining to organized crime on his way back to the shack that afternoon. Elmo made up his mind that there would be no turning back this time.

Melvin had a few errands to run in town. He dropped off their applications to the only two grocery stores that had not black-listed the boys. So many candy bars and so little time. He then stopped by the library, collected everything he could find that was gangster related, and was pulling up in their yard at a quarter to six.

"I got all the books I could find and even checked out a few movies," said Melvin, barging in the front door.

"I could hear the fire back in your voice, Elmo. What is our new venture going to be?"

That wicked and slow smile was back and spreading across Elmo's face. "Melvin, I'm sick of failure. I'm sick of life's leftovers. I'm ready for something better, and I'm taking you along for the ride. Prepare yourself for what I am about to tell you, Melvin, this could come as a shock. We are turning to a life of crime. The life of a gangster to be more exact."

"Really, Elmo, because we can't even seem to steal candy bars successfully. I'm not so sure we have got what it takes to be criminals."

"That's because we were setting our sights way too low, Melvin. We are now talking protection money, prostitution, loan sharking, murder for hire, gambling, and whatever else we can dream up. The most beautiful part is Eltonberry is virgin territory. We have no competition from other crime families. These hayseeds around here have no idea what is about to hit them. We will be wiping our butts with hundred-dollar bills before you know it. You are the only man I trust to be my number two. Are you in or out, Melvin?"

"I'm your man, Elmo, to the very end. Let's do this thing."

The rest of the night was spent poring through the books on organized crime, drinking cheap beer, and watching old gangster movies. De Niro sure made it look easy. Now, Elmo and Melvin were not the kind of guys to worry too much about details. By morning, they felt as though they were ready to tear off into the soft underbelly of the fair city of Eltonberry. The two newly ordained gangsters decided to start off with the shakedown business and protection rackets that the movies made look so easy. Just walk into a business and demand a monthly payout in exchange for "protection." If the business owner refused to pay, bad things happened.

Elmo and Melvin decided to start with the gas station on the corner of Lilly and Magnolia. Mickey's was a classy little gas station that had been around for a long time. It had been purchased the previous year by Abdul Dinari, a hard-working forty-five-year-old that had immigrated from India several years back. Since buying Mickey's station, he had put in a nice little kitchen with a hot box and several upgrades that had really boosted business. Abdul had become an American citizen and loved everything about America. That very morning, Abdul's love for America would be put to the test.

After pooling what little money they had, Elmo and Melvin had bought two very used and ill-fitting suits from a local thrift shop. The only other thing they deemed a necessity was to have a weapon of some form or fashion. Neither man owned a gun nor had enough money to buy one. Eventually, they spotted some Latino children playing baseball on a local community field.

"Watch this," said Elmo, pulling the El Camino to a stop in front of the little ball field.

Elmo casually walked up to the fence, pulled out his wallet, and started screaming, "INS, INS, INS!" The children scattered in fear at the thought of deportation, leaving all their equipment on the field. Elmo grabbed two of the aluminum baseball bats, started up the El Camino, and headed for Mickey's Gas Station.

At exactly fifteen minutes past nine o'clock in the morning, Elmo and Melvin casually strode into Mickey's. There was no one in the store at the moment but them and Abdul.

"May I help you gentlemen with anything?" asked Abdul in his thick Indian accent.

"You sure the hell can, Osama. Go fetch me one of those hundred virgins that you boys get for going to Sunday School and blowing stuff up," said Elmo with a big smirk on his face. "Let me make this really simple. We are part of a major crime family that is taking Eltonberry under its wing. Bad things are about to start happening all over the place around here. Luckily for you, a monthly donation to my favorite charity can spare your fine establishment from the trouble others will endure."

"Careful, Elmo, this boy has probably got some explosives strapped to him at this very moment," said Melvin, in his most condescending and mocking voice.

"Oh my God, you have to be kidding me," replied Abdul. "I'm not even a Muslim, you idiots. I am a Hindu from India. An Indian, not an Arab or a Muslim. Get your racism straight, please, and get out of my store. I do not find this funny at all."

"Seven one way or a dozen the other, let's not put any lipstick on this pig," replied Elmo. "You are an uneducated savage, and we haven't forgotten what you people did at the Little Bighorn either, you bastard."

"This cannot be real. No one is this stupid," replied Abdul, feeling as though he were in the middle of some strange dream. "An Indian from India, you fools. As far as education goes, I graduated at the top of my class from one of the nicest universities in India."

"Isn't that special?" asked Melvin, laughing at his poor victim. "Now you can buy yourself a teepee with a two-horse garage and a shiny new tomahawk."

"Get the hell out of my store, you fools," said Abdul, his voice cracking.

"Oh, we are going, Tonto, but first you're going to open that cash register and hand us each a hundred-dollar bill. We can offer you protection, but it isn't free," said Elmo.

"And throw in a couple of bags of chips too," added Melvin.

Abdul was starting to lose his composure and his patience, which he rarely did. After taking a really deep breath, Abdul said in his most calm voice, "I would rather die a thousand deaths than give you one copper penny."

"Melvin, take out your black book and put Chief Whistle Britches' name in it and a check by his name. It's a shame, you looked like such a bright boy." At just that moment, Elmo leaned against a large beef jerky stand, and, with two fingers, very deliberately knocked it over. Beef jerky went everywhere. At the same moment, Melvin knocked over a large pyramid of two-liter soft drinks. Out came the aluminum baseball bats from under their suit jackets. The gangsters were about to demonstrate why Abdul needed protection in the now dangerous town of Eltonberry.

Abdul was outraged. His store was covered in beef jerky and two liters, and he had taken all he was willing to take. Abdul was normally an in-control kind of guy, but something about this strange assault had pushed him past his breaking point. In a flash, Abdul had pulled out an exceptionally large .44 magnum revolver from under the counter, and he was pointing it straight at the two would-be gangsters.

"Whoa, whoa, whoa, now fella, you don't have to pull a gun on us. Put the gun away, give us the money, and we will all smoke'em peace pipe together," said Elmo, beginning to sweat profusely.

This was not the first time Abdul had been robbed, but it was the first time he had ever been so insulted by his assailants. Abdul had lived a very controlled life, and he was not prone to temper or violence of any sort. As he looked at all the beef jerky and two liters, he felt something snap inside of him, and it felt good.

"You," said Abdul, pointing the gun at Elmo. "Drop the bat and take down your pants."

"Like hell, I will," said Elmo, eyes opened wide.

"I will send you straight to hell if your pants are not down within ten seconds," said Abdul, his voice getting louder and louder.

The look in Abdul's eyes was getting crazier and crazier by the second, and Elmo was in no mood to die. He held his breath and lowered his new suit pants to the floor, revealing a pair of boxers that had seen better days. "Now take it easy there, son, I've decided I don't want your stinking money after all. Just set that gun down," said Elmo, looking over at Melvin for moral support. Melvin seemed to be frozen in some type of shock, his mouth kind of hanging open.

"It is too late for changing your mind, you fool. You brought your racist and ignorant self into my store, made a mess all over the place, and tried to rob me. Now put your hands in the air, and if you drop them, you die."

Elmo was extremely confused as he stood there with his hands in the air and his pants around his ankles. This whole thing had for sure taken a wrong turn somewhere. He had somehow very quickly lost control of this situation. Abdul now pointed the large handgun at Melvin. "You take your belt off, quickly." Melvin did as he was told, on the verge of tears. "Now, flog his ass with that belt."

"Excuse me?" shouted Elmo, very insulted. "Who the hell do you think you are?"

"I'm the crazy Indian with the gun, cowboy. Now keep your hands in the air!"

Melvin crossed his arms and refused the order. "I'd rather die than strike my friend with my own belt, and that is a fact."

Abdul fired a shot over the heads of the two men. It sounded like a cannon had gone off in the small store. The sound of the .44 magnum was so loud, it made their ears ring. Abdul looked crazier than ever as he shouted, "I said flog his ass! I will not tell you again!"

With the sound of the cannon still ringing in his ears, Melvin did not hesitate. He went to work on Elmo's ass like it was his life's calling. Melvin looked like a mad conductor leading an orchestra of the damned as he worked that belt. Melvin was a scared kind of guy to begin with, and the fear he had of that cannon going off again seemed to be a motor working that belt at top speed. Elmo screamed out with every terrible lash, but Melvin was dedicated to his work. Abdul kept urging and cheering Melvin on with each swing of the belt. Poor Elmo was full on crying with tears flooding down his face as he took the beating of his life from the best friend he had in the world. Some gangster he had turned out to be. His backside felt numb. After ten minutes or so, Abdul allowed the savage beating to stop.

"Perhaps now, you two will think twice before behaving so terribly to your fellow man. You may go on your way, I see no need to call the authorities. I am satisfied and content with your punishment."

Elmo's backside hurt so badly he could hardly stand to walk. Melvin begged his forgiveness, but Elmo couldn't even stand to look him in the eye. Back at the shack, Melvin fixed Elmo a bag of ice to sit on. It was just their luck—a De Niro marathon was on the television that night.

"I guarantee you Joe Pesci doesn't take off his belt and flog De Niro's ass at any point during this marathon," said Elmo, cutting a mean and nasty look in Melvin's direction through eyes still swollen from crying.

CHAPTER 7

Elmo gave Melvin the cold shoulder for about a week, but as the welts on his behind began to fade, so his anger faded also. Elmo called Melvin out of his room to discuss "family" business. When Melvin got to the kitchen table, he was glad to see Elmo was bubbling with excitement. Melvin started to apologize again for the beating at Abdul's gas station, but Elmo waved him off.

"Forget it, Melvin. We are an organized crime family, and there's going to be ups and downs on this journey. We have got to persevere."

"What is our next move? Are we going after Abdul again?" asked Melvin.

"No, I've got a sweeter venture planned. Charlie Williams is a low-life I know from the other side of the tracks. He works part time for that big retreat center just South of town. We were talking about places to make a buck if you weren't too worried about breaking the law and taking a few chances. Have you ever heard of the E.G.G.?"

"Yes, I scrambled a few this morning," replied Melvin, laughing.

"That is enough joking around, Melvin. Can you be serious for five flippin' minutes? The E.G.G. is the Eltonberry Golden Girls. It is a bunch of old ladies from local churches that unite and work together to raise money for the poor, orphanages, house fires, scholarships, and all kinds of crazy crap. Once a year, all the old blue hairs rent the retreat center for a weekend and have a good time fellowshipping and playing bingo or whatever. I hear they also do quite a bit of drinking while they're out there and get a little whacked out over the course of the weekend. But here is the sweet part. All the old moo cows put their jackets and purses in a little parlor room near the front door, so they don't have to keep up with them while they fellowship or drink or what not."

"So, what is the point of this story, Elmo?" asked Melvin, obviously bored already.

"The point, my idiot friend, is that Charlie Williams is going to leave the side door of the retreat center unlocked. That door opens almost directly into the parlor. The old birds start playing bingo at exactly seven o'clock. We will go in and clean out all the cash, jewelry, and credit cards that may be in those purses. They'll never know what hit them, and they will sure enough need an open bar when they find out that all their purses are empty."

"What if someone sees us?"

"Are you kidding me? Those old ladies will sit there and piss on themselves instead of going to the bathroom, so they don't miss a bingo number being called out. We will give Charlie a few dollars for the tip and unlocked door, and we are off to the races. Those old ladies do not believe in debit cards, they carry lots of cash. By the time we go to bed tonight, we will have a bundle of cash to put under our mattresses!"

The boys planned for the next few hours and spent money they did not have yet. At six o'clock, the boys had the El Camino hid in a stand of trees a couple of hundred yards away from the retreat center, but their vehicle was still close enough to the highway for a quick get-away. The retreat center was surrounded by forest and thick trees. It was a secluded area for sure, but Elmo thought that would only help them in their get-away once the crime was committed.

After almost getting lost in the now-dark forest, the boys saw the lights of the retreat center. Within minutes, they had located the side door Charlie Williams had told them about. True to his word, Charlie had the door unlocked. The boys, ever so quietly, slipped in the door, and they found, to their great delight, a massive number of purses strewn about the room. The boys had just started digging through purses when a blood-curdling scream rang out. Margie Grant was making an emergency bathroom run as fast as she could in order to get back to the bingo action when she had heard movement coming from the parlor room. Seeing what was going on, she started screaming at the top of her lungs and did not stop until the other ladies had come running to see what had happened.

Elmo and Melvin bolted out the door and into the forest. It was so dark, the woods were so thick, and the boys so panicked that they couldn't remember what direction they should be running. The sound of aluminum walking canes clanking together rang out as a small but determined army of drunken, old ladies poured out of the retreat center and into the woods fast on their trail. It was not a scenario that two relatively healthy young men would normally be too intimidated by. That began to change as the boys heard ATVs cranking up in the distance and shotguns blasting through the silence of the forest. They heard lots of profanity, followed by whooping cat calls.

"My God, these old ladies are drunk, crazy, and out of their damned minds," said Elmo as the boys tried to catch their breath for a minute while hiding in some thick brush.

"I thought these old biddies were supposed to be mild-mannered Christian grannies," whined Melvin, on the verge of tears as another shotgun blast went off.

"Well, they seem to be jacked up on Jesus and Jack Daniels at the moment. Let's just make one big run for the highway and the El Camino."

Just as the boys sprang from the bushes, one of the elderly hellhounds let out a howling whoop-whoop, and ATVs surrounded the boys within seconds. Blinded by the headlights, they never saw the lariat ropes descend over their heads. In a flash, the boys were being dragged deeper and deeper into the forest by the lariats tied to ATVs. Through briar patches, creeks, and mud holes, the boys were dragged without compassion. Each time the grannies would slow down just a little, Elmo and Melvin would try to stand up, but then the grannies would punch the gas and jerk them down again. Each time the boys were jerked back down, the grannies would burst into laughter. Mercifully, the ATVs came to a stop in a little clearing with a handful of small trees on one end.

Held at gunpoint, the boys were each tied to a tree with surprisingly strong and wrinkled hands.

"You wretched old bitches, I'm gonna kick your ancient asses when I get loose!" shouted Elmo at the top of his lungs.

Both men were covered in mud, soaking wet, and scratched up beyond belief from all the briars and rough terrain they had been dragged through. Melvin was full on crying at this point and begging to be released.

"You dare to steal from the Eltonberry Golden Girls, now you pay the price," said Clara Barton, the voice for the posse. "We wash your clothes, cook for you, raise your kids, and tolerate your wee Willy Wonkas for 60 years, and then you try and steal from us. If you hate men, give me a great big whoop-whoop!" cried out Clara, clearly very drunk.

In unison, the posse of women, never lowering their shotguns, let out a wild, "Whoop-whoop!"

A tiny blue hair with glasses that appeared to be the thickest pair ever created in the history of glasses, walked up to a tree near the boys and said, "I'll see you in hell." She unloaded her shotgun at the tree, obviously too blind to see that the boys were tied two trees away. Both boys had urinated in their pants and were full on crying as they were certain death was at hand.

"Give me that gun, Margaret," said Clara, grabbing the now-empty shotgun from the tiny woman. "You know you're blind as a bat."

"What should we do with them?" asked one of the women.

"I've always wanted to see one of those male dancer shows," said Clara, eyeing the boys up and down carefully. "We are about to cut you loose. If you want to live through the night, you are both about to shake those little backsides like your lives depend on it."

As the ropes that bound them to the trees were cut loose, Elmo started to protest their strange demand.

"Dance, monkey, dance!" screamed the drunken Clara as she fired her shotgun into the air one last time.

Both Elmo and Melvin started shaking and gyrating the best they could while covered in mud and utterly terrified. It looked a lot more like an epileptic seizure than anything else, and the old gals were laughing up a storm.

"Now one last thing, boys. Take your clothes off, and I mean all of your clothes. Don't make me say it again," demanded Clara, still holding the shotgun steady.

The boys were too afraid to argue and did as they were told. The women laughed until they decided it was time for a few more drinks. Taking the men's clothes with them, the blue-haired and drunken hellhounds mounted up on their ATVs and rode back toward the retreat center. Elmo and Melvin started the long and humiliating walk back through the woods and on to their El Camino. Covered in mosquito bites and naked as the day they were born, the two men never said a word as they walked or on the drive home. Each man silently cried himself to sleep that night.

CHAPTER 8

Neither Elmo nor Melvin wanted to discuss the night of the retreat center ever again, so they put it behind them and went on with life. True to form, about a week later, Elmo broke the news to Melvin over breakfast that it was time to move into the next phase of organized crime.

"Melvin, what is it that every man wants in this life?"

"Well, Elmo," replied Melvin, thoughtfully pondering the question, "I guess every man wants a wife to love, children, a job, and a piece of land."

"No, no, and hell no, Melvin. Every man wants a prostitute, and he wants that prostitute at a fair and reasonable price. We are opening up a cathouse right here in Eltonberry."

"That's great, I love cats," said Melvin, suddenly very excited.

"No, idiot, not real cats. I mean we are opening up Eltonberry's first whorehouse. I have already thought this whole thing out. It will be first class all the way. We will cut no corners on this project."

"Elmo, I love your energy, but I've known you since we were kids. I don't think either of us has ever actually had a real girlfriend. The point being we do not know very much about women. If you have had a girlfriend, I know you have never seen a naked woman."

"Yes, I sure as heck have. Maybe I have more experience than you think, Melvin!"

"Are you talking about the time we hid in my big sister's closet when she was changing clothes? Because you know that doesn't count. She really beat the hell out of us that night, didn't she?"

"Shut up, Melvin, and get with the program. Are you with me or not?"

"Of course, I'm with you to the end."

"Experience does not matter, this is business. We might even be able to sample the merchandise, if you know what I mean. I called my cousin in Chicago, and he is kind of plugged into the underworld over there. He agreed to ship us an entire stable of whores down here for five hundred dollars. I have a total of four hundred dollars after selling all my NASCAR memorabilia. Now, we are partners in this, Melvin. I need you to come up with the other hundred bucks."

"Dang, Elmo, I don't know. We could buy a lot of fried chicken with a hundred dollars. Have you even seen any pictures of these women that we are supposed to be getting?"

"Of course I have, Melvin. Don't insult my intelligence. Do you think I'm stupid?" asked Elmo, insulted.

Elmo pulled out the pictures his cousin had sent him. There were six pictures of extremely attractive women. Melvin was sold at first glance, and he had his hundred dollars out of his wallet and on the table within seconds of seeing the pictures. Both men were giddy with the thought of sampling the merchandise.

"I've rented old man Shipley's abandoned store on Bonner Road as our actual whorehouse. It's in rough shape, but it was cheap," said Elmo, getting more pumped up with each passing second.

"I have also passed out flyers, talked to all the bartenders, and sent word out to every no-good in and around town. You are about to be a rich man, Melvin. Let's get on over to the cathouse and start fixing it up. The women will be here at nine o'clock in the morning."

"Let's go, I'm ready," said Melvin, almost bouncing up and down.

The two men spent the rest of the night working on Mr. Shipley's old store to make it suitable for the venture at hand. The store used to be an auto parts retailer and only consisted of two rooms. There were cobwebs everywhere, and the place was in bad shape, but after working half the night, the place was a little more presentable. The boys had their waiting room, which consisted of a few folding chairs, a very small refrigerator, and a little desk. The room where business would go down consisted of a small stereo, a shower, and Elmo's own small bed which he had volunteered for the project since they could not afford a new one.

At nine o'clock the next morning, both men were looking out the window of their new cathouse. The cats should be pulling up any minute, and the house would officially open for business at six o'clock that very evening. Within a few minutes, a black van pulled up and slowed to a stop in front of the shop. The boys were so excited, they could barely contain themselves.

Elmo and Melvin ran out to meet the van. The driver of the van was a very dirty-looking sort that did not have an abundance of manners. After they exchanged a quick handshake, the driver wasted no time getting down to business. "First, the five hundred dollars, and then you get your women," said the delivery driver, as sharp and to the point as could be.

"Can we at least see the women first?" asked Melvin.

"No, we already sent you pictures. First, let's see the money. I don't have time to haggle here. Do you want to do business or not?"

"Wait a minute, calm down, mister. Here is your money," said Elmo, smiling from ear to ear. His hands were almost shaking as he handed the money to the stranger. "All right, open up the van and let me see my stable."

The stranger got in the driver's seat of the van and cranked it up. "Your three women are at the gas station on the edge of town. I'd hurry up and get over there before they start to wander."

"What the heck is going on here? I was supposed to get six women, not three."

"We went by weight instead of actual numbers."

"What the heck are you talking about, and why did you leave them at the gas station? I smell a rat here, fellow."

The stranger punched the gas and left in a fury of burnt rubber and dust with Elmo's money. Elmo was so mad that he felt like crying. But a businessman doesn't have the luxury of whining.

"Let's go get our women, Melvin. Grab the pictures they sent us so we can recognize them when we see them. Poor angels are bound to be a little nervous themselves."

When the men got out to the station, there were three women standing outside by the ice machine, but they obviously were not the women Elmo and Melvin were looking for. One of the women, who appeared to be the leader of the group, weighed at least four hundred pounds.

She had a nasty snarl and a serious skin condition. She looked like the offspring of a heavy lizard and an angry pit bull. The second lady was so skinny she hardly looked alive. Her nose was the heaviest thing on her body and was so large that a grown man could take refuge underneath it in a rainstorm and never get wet. Four large warts had made themselves at home on the left side of her face. The third and final lady was a bit confusing to look at. She was extremely hairy and muscular with several missing teeth. She wore an eye-patch just like a pirate and had an Adam's apple the size of a softball. She looked very masculine to say the least.

As Elmo got out of the car, he approached the ladies and held out the pictures for them to see, "Excuse me, ladies, have you seen any of these women around here in the last little bit?"

"Yes, that's us," said the big one in a very short, deep, and to the point kind of way.

"The hell you say," said Elmo, feeling a sick feeling creep over him.

"Are you blind or what?" asked the big woman. "Of course that's us in those pictures. Now, we are hungry. What are you going to do about it?"

Elmo held up one of the pictures beside the big woman's face. "Lady, if the woman in this picture had been hit by a train, contracted typhoid fever, and found herself pregnant with triplets, she still would not resemble you. You ain't in any of these pictures, big'un."

The woman was surprisingly quick as she reached out and put a huge hand around Elmo's throat, lifted him off the ground a little, and said through gritted teeth, "If your name is Elmo Bogg, then we are the whores you ordered. My name is Big Sue, and if we are going to work for you, then you are going to have to feed us. I have a blood sugar condition, and I don't like to be kept waiting when it comes to my meals. Are we clear?"

Big Sue's grip was impressive, and Elmo could barely get any air to speak with. He finally managed a weak yes, and Big Sue let him go. Elmo cussed his no-good cousin and his rotten luck for about ten minutes. After he had kicked enough dirt and let out enough vulgarities, he told the women to get in the back of the El Camino, but they insisted on riding in the front. An El Camino only has enough room for two people and a bed like a truck in the back, so this meant Melvin had to ride in the back of the car. Melvin was very happy not to be squeezed up front with Elmo and Elmo's new stable of women.

As they headed for Bob's Barbeque to get Big Sue and the girls some ribs, Elmo realized just how terrible the women smelled. It was such an overpowering stench, he had to hold his head out the window as he drove. They got the ribs to go and headed for the cathouse.

When they got back to the cathouse, Big Sue literally attacked the ribs like a lion on a wounded deer. The two other women carefully reached in the pan and came out with one rib each. Big Sue seemed to almost growl as they did so.

Elmo and Melvin stepped outside to talk in private, "God help us all, Elmo, this is turning into a bad dream. We are not going to make any money with those three, and you know it," said Melvin in a hushed tone so the women could not hear.

"Look, Melvin, I know this looks bad, but we have already invested the five hundred dollars, rented this shop, and advertised all over town. We are broke man, we can't stop now. Maybe, we could turn the lights down really low, and the fellows won't get a real good look at them."

"Elmo, I'm not even positive that hairy one is a woman. I heard it growl earlier when I walked by it. The big one passed gas a few minutes ago, and I almost passed out. The skinny one smells like she has not taken a shower in years, or maybe ever."

"Look, Melvin, shut up. If you can't be positive, just keep your mouth shut. I am not giving up on this dream. I have been praying a lot about this, and I have a feeling God is going to bless our little whorehouse before this is over, despite our bad luck. I saw two old cats humping in the alley beside Bob's Barbeque earlier, and I took it as a good omen. I want you to go to the supermarket and pick up some soap, deodorant, perfume, lipstick, lots of makeup, some gas pills, and some really weak light bulbs. Shoplift if you have to."

"Can I grab a candy bar while I'm at it?" asked Melvin.

"Whatever, just hurry up! And grab some kind of romantic mood music. I'll stay here and try to get these three to take a good shower."

Elmo had laid down the ground rules to his stable and insisted they each take a long shower before opening night. Big Sue had passed wind four more times over the course of the afternoon, and it was mind-boggling to think that a human being could smell that bad. Elmo had threatened Big Sue with a beating if she didn't stop the farting, but she just growled and snarled. Elmo knew that on the best day of his life, he couldn't whip Big Sue, but he had to try to get his bluff in. The three girls had one suitcase between them that held one change of clothes for each of them. The showers helped a little with the smell, but the smell was not giving up its hold on the women easily. Big Sue kept right on farting at regular intervals, and then denying it even though it sounded like Abdul's .44 magnum going off in the small cathouse. Elmo had to go outside for air multiple times.

Big Sue came to Elmo after her shower and demanded something to eat.

"My God, I just fed you a pan full of ribs not three hours ago," said Elmo amazed and in shock.

"That was yesterday," said Big Sue.

"The hell you say," said Elmo. "I only first met you a little over three hours ago this very day. No wonder you are so huge."

Her quickness was as breath-taking as her farts. Big Sue once again had Elmo by the throat and was slowly squeezing. "I said I'm hungry right now. Do you understand the words coming out of my mouth, little man?"

Poor Elmo could not even speak, so he just nodded his head. He called in an order for a large pizza to be delivered for Big Sue. As he looked in his almost-empty wallet, he knew these women better start making him some money soon. At the rate Big Sue was eating, they would all be on welfare quick if the business was a bust.

Melvin got back and handed out deodorant, makeup, perfume, and lipstick. The smell got just a little better with the deodorant and some scented candles burning. The makeup did not do a lot for their looks. It was like trying to hide a killer whale in a swimming pool. When Elmo and Melvin went to inspect the women, they noticed the skinny one had actually eaten her lipstick. Her teeth were bright red, and there was red all over the bottom half of her face. She was hissing like a snake and smiling in a strange and foreboding way.

"God help us," said Elmo as he examined the three women. "We need a busload of horny, blind men with strong stomachs. You want to sample the merchandise, Melvin?"

"Not on your life. I'd rather drink broken glass."

"Me too," said Elmo, fighting back tears.

CHAPTER 9

At six o'clock on the dot, there was a knock at the door. Elmo opened the door and welcomed their first client inside. Andrew Smith was a mechanic and known around town as a scoundrel. As Elmo led him into the waiting room, he had the three women line up.

"Take your pick, Mr. Smith. For fifty dollars, all your dreams can come true this very night," said Elmo.

Andrew Smith had been smiling on the way to the cathouse, he was smiling as he pulled up to the cathouse, and he was smiling as he walked into the cathouse. As he looked at his three choices, Andrew Smith was not smiling anymore.

For just a minute, there was absolute silence in the room. Andrew slowly cleared his throat for a minute as he stared at the floor, and he suddenly remembered he loved his wife and needed to get home. "Is this the lamp store? Because I thought this was a lamp shop. I think there has been some mistake here," said Andrew, backing away towards the door.

"Wait, Andrew, I can come down in price!" shouted Elmo, but it was too late. Their first client was gone. Over the next couple of hours, five more potential clients came in smiling and left as soon as they laid eyes on Elmo's so-called stable of women.

Elmo was about ready to call it quits as it neared midnight, but then there was another knock at the door. Elmo opened the door to see Caleb Jackson. Caleb was notorious around Eltonberry for having no decency in him at all. Caleb was a huge guy and had to almost duck to get in the door. He was also very versed in the ways of the world. Elmo was delighted to see him. If anyone would roll around with his gals, it would be Caleb. As Caleb stared at his three choices, he had a sick look on his face.

"Elmo, I ain't a picky man, you understand, but damn it, boy, this is hard to swallow," said Caleb. "Every man's got a line in the sand. How much money?"

Elmo decided to drop the price to twenty-five dollars, but Caleb started for the door. Elmo dropped the price three more times before Caleb got to the door, but Caleb still wasn't biting. "All right, Caleb, I'm going to do something special for you. For one dollar, you can have any one of these women, and then you can help spread the word around town for us. We will let you kind of prime the pump on our little cathouse, so to speak."

Now, Caleb had been sure he was leaving, but not even he could say no to one dollar. Caleb held his head down in shame and took one green dollar out of his wallet. He timidly held it out to Elmo. Elmo smiled and reached for the dollar. Just as Elmo's fingers touched the dollar, Big Sue let out a ringing fart that filled the place like an invading army and seemed to echo throughout the cathouse. Caleb yanked the dollar back and shouted, "Hell no! I will not defile myself here tonight. Not with that anyway!" Caleb shouted, pointing toward the women.

Elmo tried to grab Caleb's wrist and pry the dollar out, shouting something about a verbal contract, but Caleb slapped Elmo a ringing blow, sending him flying to the floor. Melvin picked up a tire tool, ready to defend Elmo, but Caleb was gone.

Elmo jumped up, furious. "Big Sue, I warned you about that farting! Did you take the anti-gas pill or not? You ignorant bitches have got to start earning!" screamed Elmo.

Now, it was not clear whether it was the ignorant remark or the bitches remark, but Big Sue came after Elmo at a dead run. She ripped his shirt open and off as she slammed him around the small room, and then she unbuckled his belt. For a moment, Elmo was terrified he was about to be violated, but she just ripped his belt loose from his pants and proceeded to give Elmo the beating of a lifetime. He screamed out in agony. Melvin jumped on her back, trying to stop her, but she threw him like a small child against one of the walls. She beat Elmo until she had no more energy left, and then she and her two comrades left like phantom whores into the night. Elmo just laid there and cried. Melvin tried to comfort him, but Elmo was beside himself with grief. There were large welts all over his back, his belly, his face, and his poor behind. It was like a bad dream as the two men laid on the floor and moaned. You would have never known the whores were there except for the terrible smell they left behind.

CHAPTER 10

Elmo and Melvin were devastated that their venture into the skin trade had been such a monumental failure. Shakedowns and prostitution were obviously not going to pay the rent. They were still intent on being gangsters, so that only left one terrible avenue open. The two men were going to have to look into killing for money. Murder for hire was heavy stuff, but it had come to this.

They put the word out on the street that "problems" could be made to "go away" if anyone was in need of their services. Within a few days, an acquaintance gave Elmo the tip that there was a local farmer with need of their particular services. Elmo and Melvin took a deep breath, loaded up in the El Camino, and headed for old man Henderson's farm.

As they pulled up in the driveway, Mr. Henderson was in the front yard fixing an old birdhouse that the wind had wreaked havoc on. "Hello, Mr. Henderson, my name is

Elmo Bogg and this is Melvin Perkins. We understand you have a problem that we might be able to make go away for you."

"Are you the boys my nephew called for me?"

"Yes, sir. Arnold didn't tell us any details though."

"Well," replied Mr. Henderson, thoughtfully. "It is no doubt illegal in this day and age to take care of one's 'problems' this way. We used to do it all the time when I was younger. The law used to let a man be a man without trying to lock him up all the time. The old bitch is tied up in the backyard. I care for her deeply, but she has been screwing around at the neighbor's barn every time I turn around. I just cannot tolerate it anymore. Take her off somewhere else to do the deed. I care for her way too much to do it myself, but this going over to the neighbor's place has got to stop. I will always have feelings for her, but she is really old. I guess I just need something younger that can keep up with the workload around here on the farm anyway. Be as gentle with her as you can, boys, and bury her when it is over."

"Don't you worry about a thing, Mr. Henderson, we will take care of everything. It will cost you five hundred dollars, though. Are you okay with that?"

"You are out of your dad-gum mind. I'll do it myself if it costs more than twenty-five dollars."

Elmo and Melvin reluctantly agreed and took Mr. Henderson's cash. As they walked around the back of the house, Mrs. Henderson was trying to untie some knots out of a clothesline rope right by the back door. Elmo and Melvin raced over and grabbed her by the arm. "Not so fast, granny, you've got to come with us. Almost got away, didn't you?" asked Elmo.

Mrs. Henderson was even older than Mr. Henderson, and she was a very timid and soft-spoken soul. She did not put up much of a fight at all. She just kept saying, "Oh my, oh, my…"

"Granny, you shouldn't have been fooling around with the neighbor if you didn't want to pay the piper. Let's go. Get in the car, and this can be relatively painless," said Elmo.

Elmo had her by one arm, and Melvin had her by the other. They were frog marching her out to the El Camino when Mr. Henderson caught sight of them. He charged them like an angry bull. As he ran, he grabbed a thick piece of cotton rope laying on the front porch and commenced to putting a heck of a beating on the two would-be hitmen. After he was out of breath to the point that he could not continue the beating, he shouted, "You fools, that's my wife! I meant the dog tied to the back fence. Ten years ago, I would have killed you both for this! Get off my place, and take the dog with you!" shouted Mr. Henderson, giving the boys one more dirty look. He put a loving arm around his wife and gently led her back toward the house.

Fifteen minutes later, the two men were back on the road with an old, black dog sitting in between them. "That could have got really ugly," said Melvin. "He'd still be beating on us if we had killed that old woman. He probably would have taken back the twenty-five dollars too."

"Let's concentrate on the job at hand," said Elmo.

They stopped at Miller's bridge, which stood a good seventy feet over a fast-moving river. The river had lots of sharp and jagged rocks sprinkled throughout. Elmo untied the dog and started trying to heave it up over the side of the iron bridge. "Give me a hand, Melvin."

"What are you doing? Are you crazy?" shouted Melvin.

"Melvin, we took the man's money and told him we would kill this dog. I'm just glad it's not old Mrs.

Henderson's ass we are about to throw over the side of this bridge. I knew you would get squeamish when it was time to do the deed."

"All right, all right, it just seems cruel."

"Well, remember, we do not own a gun and can't afford one. Now give me a hand, and it will all be over in just a minute."

Melvin reluctantly helped Elmo. The poor old hound never made a sound all the way down. The two men slowly peered over the side of the bridge, and, to their amazement, the old dog was swimming for the shore. She made it to safety and made a beeline right back to Elmo's feet. Elmo and Melvin just kind of stared at each other and then at the wet dog at their feet. Not sure exactly what to do, they picked her up and threw her over a second time. This time she hit some of the rocks, and they heard a splat. As they peered over the bridge, they were in utter shock to see the dog limping off the rocks and swimming back to shore where she limped right back up to Elmo and Melvin's feet. Melvin had begun to cry a little bit, so Elmo just put the dog back in the El Camino and headed for home.

When they got home, Elmo explained to Melvin that the plan was still in motion. They were just going to have to kill the dog in some other fashion. Elmo picked up a hammer and handed it to Melvin.

"What is this for?" asked Melvin.

"Hit her right between the eyes. You're my right-hand man, aren't you?"

"Not today," said Melvin, throwing the hammer on the ground and crossing his arms. "You do it yourself."

Elmo grabbed the hammer up, aimed it just so at the old dog's head, and he hit it right between the eyes. The dog dropped like it had been shot. It jerked its legs a little in the agony of death. Elmo and Melvin bowed their heads in reverence and remorse. Suddenly, the dog jumped back up, walked back over to Melvin, and sat down by his feet. The men were starting to get an eerie feeling that maybe this dog was not meant to die.

"We have got to try one more thing, Melvin. Tie the dog in the middle of the driveway. I'm going to run her over with the El Camino."

Melvin was full out ugly crying at this point.

"I'm sorry, Melvin. I hate this too! I take no pleasure in this at all, but it is just business. It is nothing personal against the dog. Remember, Mr. Henderson said she was old and pretty sick."

After hugging the dog's neck and crying a bit more, Melvin tied the dog like Elmo had instructed. Elmo revved up the engine, put it in gear, and hit the dog at a good rate of speed. The dog went flying, and both men knew the deed was done. The dog flew a good thirty feet through the air and lay motionless in the grass. Now, both men were crying. They had to admire a fighter. Melvin began to try to sing a few lines of "Amazing Grace," and Elmo bowed his head out of respect.

As the two men were singing and crying, the old dog got back up one more time and dragged itself between them. As they finished their song and looked down, they both got down and hugged the dog tight. They adopted the dog right there on the spot. The duo was now a trio. "Screw Mr. Henderson, and we're keeping the money too," said Elmo. Both men saw a little bit of themselves in the old, black dog. Sometimes there wasn't anything to do but just keep getting back up.

CHAPTER 11

E lmo and Melvin had hit upon hard times. No matter how hard they worked at making their fortune, they could find no success. On top of everything else, the local mud races were about to kick off. It was an annual event where everyone went out to a dirt track and watched tricked-out four wheelers get down and dirty in all manner of terrible mud holes. Everyone tried to drink their own weight in beer. It was a blast for all that attended. Elmo and Melvin were faithful attendees at the event every year, but this year they were flat broke. All their money had been blown on the renegade prostitutes in a scheme that had made them exactly zero dollars. Mafia Don Elmo and his second in command had failed terribly as would-be gangsters, and the money from their final grocery store check was long gone.

The guys were sitting around their kitchen table and brainstorming when Elmo came up with an idea that got his blood pumping again. "Melvin, do you remember when we were in high school, and we were saving up for the subscription to that dirty magazine? We came up with that scam where we panhandled and acted like you had a rare disease of the mind. We ended up making good money on that one. What if we just took it to another level?"

"I hated that scam. You made me slobber the entire day."

"Yes, I did, but our profit margin was directly tied to how much slobber you could produce. Do you want to go to the mud races or not?" asked Elmo.

Elmo made out a list and used the last few dollars they had to pick up the supplies needed for the venture at hand. The men decided not to poop in their own backyard; they would go about forty miles away to the town of Fullerton to pull off their scam. Elmo went in by himself to pick up the supplies at the drugstore. He closely guarded the bag when he got back in the car, which irritated Melvin to no small degree. Melvin had the same bad feeling in his gut that always preceded one of Elmo's extra bad ideas.

As they drove on to Fullerton, Elmo just sat very quietly and stared forward with a serious look on his face. Melvin was beside himself with anxiety, he knew this was about to get ugly. Elmo pulled into a parking lot near a large trash dumpster and killed the El Camino. "Melvin, I'm just going to be completely honest with you. I'm not going to sugar-coat what is ahead of us. This venture is going to take a big commitment on your part. It will be terrible for a few hours, and then we will go home with pockets full of money ready for the races. I can almost taste the beer and the mud now. The money we make today will make this year's mud races the best ever for us."

"Spit it out, Elmo, or I'm going home. What is the plan?" demanded Melvin.

"I need you to take all your clothes off and put on one of these," said Elmo, pulling out a small pack of adult diapers. "You are going to decide right now whether you're my right-hand man or not. I'd do it for you in a heartbeat."

"That is the darn point, Elmo, it is never you. It's always me."

"Melvin, I would do it if I could pull it off like you, but you play the part of a man with mental problems to a point of perfection. I'm talking you could win an Oscar when you really get going. It is almost as if you really are a man with mental problems."

Fifteen minutes later, when he saw he could not prevail, Melvin took the adult diaper and walked behind the dumpster. Five more minutes and Melvin stepped out from behind the dumpster wearing nothing but the diaper. Melvin was too ashamed to look up, but his loyalty was greater than his shame. Elmo took out a chocolate bar and demanded that Melvin put it in the diaper so it could start getting nice and hot. Melvin started to cry as Elmo explained the scam in more detail.

"You can go through the motions, and we can make a little money, or you can put your heart into this thing, and we can make a lot of money. Just remember you only have a few things to do as the ladies come out of the grocery store. Don't approach any men, or we could end up getting our butts kicked. I'll do all the talking," said Elmo, giddy with excitement. "It's go time!"

An hour later, they were positioned outside the front door of Fullerton's biggest grocery store. As the ladies would come out of the grocery store, Elmo began explaining about the surgery his little brother needed in order to be normal again. Melvin would grunt and slobber and fall down ever so often. Every few minutes, per

Elmo's instructions, Melvin would scream out at things that were not there or shriek out like an African big cat. Elmo tried not to micromanage. He allowed Melvin to pick out which cat he was feeling at the moment. Elmo had a long rope tied around Melvin's waist. If the ladies gave generously, all was well. If the ladies refused to give or tried to just dump a little change on them, Melvin would step it up to the next level. The chocolate bar was good and melted in his diaper, and he would reach down into the diaper and pull his hand out with melted chocolate all over it, stretch his arms straight out, and walk toward the ladies like a small child walking to its mother. The two men had positioned themselves in such a way that the ladies were kind of pinned between the brick wall of the grocery store and Melvin's outstretched chocolate hands. Elmo would make a big show of trying to pull Melvin back by the rope to no avail.

The sheer panic on the faces of the women at the site of Melvin lumbering toward them was something to never forget. "He only calms down when he sees enough cash go in the bucket!" shouted Elmo, pretending to fight with and pull on the rope. The women began to just turn their purses over and pour cash into the bucket which would, of course, calm down the lumbering chocolate hands. The women would have taken out another mortgage on their homes to avoid the chocolate hands.

After an hour or so, Elmo's bucket was literally brimming with cash. Even Melvin had really gotten into it, and he was playing the part to perfection. Ever so often, Elmo would slip another chocolate candy bar into Melvin's diaper. It looked like the men might be able to retire by the time the day was over. Elmo had to go out to the car and dump their bucket twice. It was a thing of twisted beauty.

CHAPTER 12

Officers Hillshire and Smith were just sitting down to a fine breakfast when the call came across their radios. There was trouble at Fullerton Market. The police officers asked their waitress to put their plates back under the heat lamp while they went to take care of a little bit of police business. Pissed off, the officers got in their car and headed for the pan-handling problem that had just been called in from dispatch.

"Really pisses me off," said Officer Smith as they pulled into the parking lot of Fullerton Market. "These losers are too lazy to get a real job. A man can't even eat his darn breakfast," complained Officer Smith. Officer Hillshire nodded in agreement.

Now, Officer Hillshire had some secrets that the average acquaintance might not know. Officer Hillshire had been on vacation for the last two weeks, but that was just a cover story. John Hillshire had been in a lockdown facility trying to get help for a problem that had haunted him for the better part of his entire life. John Hillshire was terrified of germs. It was not a casual fear. It was the kind of fear that had brought him to the brink of disaster many times. He could not even have a girlfriend, it was so bad. Bodily fluids, human touch, coughing, sneezing, and fecal matter were the stuff his nightmares were made of.

The law officers easily spotted Elmo as they pulled up to the scene, but Melvin was not in sight because of the angle they were approaching from. "Let's put the fear of God in this putz and get back to breakfast," said Hillshire as they parked their car and walked up on the scene. Elmo spotted the approaching officers as they were about twenty feet away.

"Melvin, we got the fuzz on our butts!" shouted Elmo.

"What do we do now?" asked Melvin, his knees starting to shake.

"Melvin, reach in that diaper one last time and charge these old boys while I get away with the money. I'll meet you at the fairgrounds in one hour. There is no time to ponder this. Reach in that diaper and charge them or we lose all our money!"

As Officer Hillshire got closer and Melvin, wearing nothing but that diaper, came into view, he froze in absolute fear. It would have been better for him if Melvin had been holding a rocket launcher. He could see brown stuff all over Melvin's hands. Of all the things Officer Hillshire struggled with, nothing compared to fecal matter. And then it happened. It almost appeared to Officer Hillshire to be in slow motion. Melvin reached in the diaper, cleaned out what was left of the chocolate, and charged the officers like Braveheart on crack.

Officer Hillshire let out a blood-curdling scream that was heard by everyone for miles in every direction. Hillshire pulled out his police-issue mace and began spraying it wildly in Melvin's direction. Melvin took the blast directly in the face. Now blinded, Melvin continued his desperate charge toward Officer Hillshire who started backpedaling into the Fullerton Market. Hillshire kept spraying the mace and screaming like something out of a horror movie. Officer Smith was unnerved by his partner's piercing screams. He was way out of shape, but was running the best he could in hot pursuit of his screeching partner. Hillshire ended up spraying several shoppers with mace as he was spraying it at Melvin. Out of mace, Officer Hillshire turned around and took off at a dead run down the underwear aisle. Melvin was now completely blind and just running forward, still with hands covered in chocolate and outstretched toward anything and anybody in his way. A rather large woman looked up just in time to get a chocolate hand in her face as Melvin raced by. She took a swing at Melvin, missed, and fainted in the aisle. Officer Smith, chasing after Melvin and his partner, tripped on the fat woman with chocolate on her face.

Officer Hillshire was screaming out for Jesus to help him because Melvin had still not stopped his blind charge. Hillshire pulled his taser out and shot at Melvin, but ended up hitting an elderly man on a walker who went down instantly. They were almost at the back wall of the supermarket, which meant Officer Hillshire was cornered. The unstoppable Melvin was still coming. Knowing he would rather die, lose his job, and burn in hell rather than be touched by the poo-poo hands, he did the only thing he could think to do.

Officer Hillshire, without hesitation, pulled out his service revolver and started squeezing off live rounds. Two jars of pickles, a box of rice, and a can of baked beans were shot in the gunfire, but amazingly, Melvin was not injured. Officer Smith's police hat was shot right off his head by one of the bullets whizzing by. Neither of the police officers were thinking about breakfast anymore, that was for darn sure.

Officer Hillshire hit the back wall of the store and turned around just in time to see Melvin's brown hands outstretched. The brown hands caught him right in the face. Instantly, Officer Hillshire became absolutely hysterical. Melvin was exhausted and lay down on the floor, still blind and choking on mace. Officer Smith tried desperately to calm his partner down to no avail. Hillshire was screaming at the top of his lungs. It got so bad that Officer Smith eventually had to tase his own partner in order to keep him from reloading his revolver and going after Melvin again. Needless to say, Melvin was handcuffed and taken to the county jail.

Elmo had almost gotten out of Fullerton with the money, but an alert state trooper caught and arrested him after listening to the description of the fleeing car. When Elmo got to jail, he had been worried that someone might have already molested poor Melvin, but as it turned out, he had nothing to worry about. The large holding cell was filled with killers, rapists, thieves, and cut-throats, but they were all huddled on one side of the large cell. Poor little Melvin, still wearing nothing but an adult diaper, blinded, eyes swollen, and hands still covered in brown sat all by himself on the other side of the cell. He was moaning and weeping as Elmo went in and sat beside him.

"Melvin, I have never been prouder of you than I am at this very moment," said Elmo, putting his arm around Melvin's shoulders. "You truly are my right-hand man."

A huge biker from the other side of the cell winced in terror as Melvin's chocolate hand slid across Elmo's face, leaving a large brown smear.

CHAPTER 13

Elmo and Melvin had been in the holding cell about two hours when Judge Clayton was escorted to the cell by one of the officers. He motioned for Elmo to come over to the cell door. "Elmo, I understand you and Melvin have been breaking the law and raising all kinds of hell over here in our neighboring county. What do you have to say for yourself, son?"

"Well," replied Elmo, sheepishly, "I really can't think of a good excuse, so I'll try the truth. We need some money, Judge. I know it was stupid, but it all kind of seemed harmless at the time."

"Here is the bottom line, Elmo. You and your little friend over there in the diaper are in a lot of trouble. I knew your old grandfather when we were much younger men. He helped me out a few times when he didn't have to, and I hate to see you spend years of your life in a jail cell. You're not exactly built for self-preservation inside of prison, son. I mean, you are looking at real jail time here. But there could be another way out of this if you were interested. You see, my father is an elderly man, and he's rather difficult to deal with. His full-time nurse is out of town on a little vacation for the next two weeks, and his temporary nurse just quit on me this very afternoon. Most of the nurses anywhere remotely close by have already sworn off having anything to do with my father as he can be a special kind of challenge at times. I have a very important job, and I cannot afford to miss work right now. This leaves me in a pickle. What would you think about looking after him for a few days until I can make other arrangements?"

"I'd be happy to help you out, Judge, but it appears I'm about to face the long arm of the law."

"I can call in a favor and make this go away if you're interested in watching my father. Now, I'm serious when I tell you that my father is not a kind or good man. He's eighty-two years old, and he is just as mean as an old snake. Are you up for it?"

"I'm your man, Judge. Of course, I'll need you to get my partner in crime out also. I couldn't live with myself if he had to stay in here."

"Done," replied Judge Clayton. "Be at my house tomorrow morning at seven o'clock."

Within the hour, Elmo and Melvin were in their El Camino headed back for Eltonberry. All their ill-gotten gain had been confiscated, but at least they felt fortunate to avoid jail over the whole matter. Melvin's eyes were still swollen shut from the mace, and he was giving Elmo the silent treatment all the way home.

"Melvin, I feel rotten about the way this all worked out for you. You just take the next few days off and relax. I'll watch this old fart, and we can put this whole episode behind us."

The next morning, Elmo rang Judge Clayton's doorbell at exactly seven o'clock. The judge welcomed Elmo into his home and brought him into the living room where a nice-looking elderly man was sitting on the couch with his coffee and newspaper. Judge Clayton introduced Elmo to his father, Mr. Bull Clayton, and then asked Elmo to step outside with him for a moment. "Elmo, I know he looks like a harmless old man, but he's not. He is an old rascal, and, at times, he's a lot worse than that. You are not to drink anything he would hand you, do not eat anything he fixes, he is not to leave this house under any circumstances, do not leave your keys laying around, don't turn your back on him, and do not fall asleep in the same house with that old man."

"My goodness, Judge, is that your father or Hannibal Lector in there?" asked Elmo, laughing. He can't be that bad. You go on to work and relax. We will be fine, I promise."

"You better take my advice seriously, Elmo. I will be back between five and six this evening. If you need me, I left my numbers on a tablet by the phone. Good luck, Elmo. You're probably going to wish I would have left you back in that jail cell before this is all over."

Elmo went back in the house and started making conversation with the old man who seemed much nicer than Judge Clayton had described. He was talking politely and being friendly, but Elmo had the feeling that he was being sized up by the old gentleman. A couple of times Elmo had a shiver go up his spine when he made eye contact with the old fellow.

"This is embarrassing, son, but I need to go have a bowel movement. I guess my son told you that I am paralyzed from the waist down and in my hands as a result of my serving in World War Two."

"Oh my God, I didn't realize that. Judge Clayton didn't mention anything about that. Do you have a wheelchair I can help you get in?"

"Yes," replied the old man thoughtfully. "But my chair is in the shop getting worked on right now. I'm afraid you're going to have to carry me in there and help me take care of my business."

"No, I did not sign up for bathroom duty. I better call your son about this."

"Damn it, there's not time for that. I am about to shit all over myself if you don't help me right now," said the old man, doubled over and clutching his stomach.

"Oh hell, all right. Let's go."

Elmo walked over to the couch, and using all the strength he had, he picked up Bull Clayton like a small baby and carried him into the bathroom. After almost falling twice due to Bull being such a large guy, they finally made it to the toilet. Bull made Elmo take down his pants and shorts and position him just so on the seat. Due to his vertigo, Bull needed Elmo to hold him steady on the toilet, or he would fall over. Bull punished the toilet with what sounded like demonic diarrhea. The smell was gut-wrenching as he stood beside the grunting Bull Clayton and held him by the arm. Elmo held his breath and prayed to God for this nightmare to end. When he was finally finished, Bull hit Elmo with the terrible news. "You're going to have to wipe my ass, son. I'm so ashamed to ask, but I just can't do it," said the old man.

"The hell you say," said Elmo, suddenly serious as a heart attack.

"You know my hands are paralyzed, you ungrateful whelp! I suffered these wounds making sure you didn't have to grow up speaking German or Japanese. I'm not wearing this mess on my backside all day. Do your job, boy!"

"Fartin' frogs, this ain't right!" shouted Elmo.

Elmo finally took a deep breath and gave up the fight. He felt like he could pass out at any moment, the smell was so incredibly bad. Elmo managed to lean the old man forward, but it was extremely hard to balance his weight and wipe at the same time. Every time Elmo would try to wipe, the old man would start a strange shaking and Elmo would get a little poop on his hand. "My God!" Elmo screamed out, starting to cry just a little. "Hold still, you're getting it on my hand! It smells like something has crawled up in your ass and died," said Elmo, covered in sweat and on the verge of passing out. Elmo was suddenly hit with a case of the dry heaves as he could not bear the stench anymore. Just before he lost his breakfast, he finished up and ran out of the bathroom for some fresh air. "Give me just a minute, Mr. Clayton, and I'll come carry you back to the couch," said Elmo, still trying to calm down and catch his breath.

"That's okay, boy, I've got it under control," said Bull Clayton, standing up on his own two feet. He pulled his pants up and buttoned them with very strong and healthy hands. He then walked, almost strutted, back toward the couch and began to dance around in a circle with his fists clenched in pure joy. He finally eased down on the couch with a smile on his face, utterly fulfilled and content.

Elmo just stood there with his mouth wide open in disbelief. His hands were shaking. Elmo grabbed a small clock off the bookshelf and threw it at Bull. Bull caught it in one hand and whizzed it straight back at Elmo. The clock hit Elmo in the temple, and he dropped to the floor like a ton of bricks. As he lay on the floor holding his head, the realization that he was in the presence of pure evil filled his mind as the sounds of an old man's hysterical laughter filled his ears.

CHAPTER 14

Elmo had to keep his distance from the old man for a while. He had visions of strangling the old fart for a good two hours. For lunch, Elmo made the old man a grilled cheese. Bull ate most of the sandwich and leaned back in his chair. "That was a good sandwich. You cook good. That's the sign of a queer, a fellow that cooks good. I bet you do laundry and sew too."

"You really are an evil old man. I wish I'd sprinkled rat poison on that grilled cheese. There is nothing gay about me either, for your information. I've had hundreds of girlfriends," said Elmo.

"Is that right? I'd bet my last dollar you live with another man. Am I right?" asked Bull, breaking out into that wicked laughter that came from somewhere deep within.

"His name is Melvin, and he is my roommate."

"I bet he is. I bet you prairie-fairies have kissed in every room you've got."

Bull erupted into more laughter, and Elmo just walked out of the room, hoping Bull would choke on what was left of the grilled cheese. For a few hours, they had an uneasy truce. Elmo was finally starting to relax around the old man just a little as they sat in the living room and read magazines. Bull started to stand up, but he stopped and asked Elmo to go get his cane out of the hall closet because his back was stove up from sitting so long. Elmo did as he was asked. As Bull stood up, he dropped his inhaler. Elmo bent over to pick it up and felt a tremendous thud hit him in the back of the head. Elmo remembered a spinning sensation, and then everything went dark. When Elmo finally woke up, it took a few minutes to regain his composure and get up off the floor. He saw that Bull was gone and the front door was wide open.

As Elmo ran to the door, he also noticed that his pants pocket was completely ripped open and just hanging from the side of his jeans. His keys and the El Camino were gone. Panic was setting in as he ran to get the phone number Judge Clayton had left by the phone, but when he called it, he got the girls of many nations phone sex line. Elmo went outside and ran to the closest neighbor's house, which was a good mile down the road. When he got there, the neighbor was able to get ahold of a very agitated Judge Clayton, who happened to be in the middle of a very important trial.

"Elmo, I should have left you in that jail cell, boy. Tell Mrs. Anderson to let you borrow their old work truck and go find that old man before he ends up in jail himself. Move your butt!"

Elmo took off for town and saw a commotion outside Eltonberry's only pharmacy. He parked the truck and ran inside. Elmo asked one of the men standing in the pharmacy what the fuss was about. The man informed

Elmo that some old guy had come in and robbed the place, but all he took was a big bottle of whiskey and some Viagra.

"Oh my God in heaven," whispered Elmo as he ran back to his truck. He was speeding up and down all the side streets in town when he spotted his El Camino parked outside Live Oaks Rehabilitation Center. He ran inside where Officer John Hillshire was taking a police report from the head of nursing. Officer Hillshire had been transferred to Eltonberry for his own safety after spraying mace on, tasing, and almost killing several people in Fullerton as a result of Melvin's chocolate hands. The people of Fullerton wanted him gone, and Judge Clayton had got him a position with the Eltonberry police force. Luckily, Officer Hillshire didn't recognize Elmo as he was intently taking Nurse Betty Blithe's statement about the terror that had just visited Live Oaks. Elmo stood back, but he listened closely as she went through the story.

"This old man runs inside with a half-empty whiskey bottle, swallows a handful of pills, and begins to sexually assault everyone he can chase down. He felt up two old ladies and a slow-moving nurse before we were able to get a male orderly up here. He bashes the mail orderly over the head with his cane and takes off into the parking lot, squealing like a madman. His El Camino wouldn't start so he runs up to Mrs. Broxton, who is in the parking lot sitting on her motorized rascal scooter. She is calmly having a smoke. He bear hugs her, throws her to the ground, takes the half-smoked cigarette from her mouth, and takes off down the street, headed east on her motorized scooter. I might add he was still chugging on that whiskey bottle while he was driving Mrs. Broxton's scooter," reported the old nurse.

"How fast would you say this rascal can go, ma'am?" asked Officer Hillshire.

"I would guess about two miles per hour if you were really pedal to the medal, but I don't know."

Elmo didn't wait around to hear any more. He and Officer Hillshire pulled out of the parking lot at the same time. Elmo let the police car take the lead, and it did not take long before they were right behind Bull Clayton as he was swerving to and fro. He tried to knock a mailbox over with his cane, but couldn't get the job done. Officer Hillshire pulled up right beside Bull and was trying to talk him into pulling the rascal over when Bull, without warning, leaned over and spit through Officer Hillshire's open window. Officer Hillshire screamed like a woman as the saliva hit him. He instantly swerved the police car over and into a telephone pole. He jumped out of the wrecked car and took off at a dead run, still screaming with spit hanging from his cheek.

Now Elmo was up. He drove on up ahead of the slow-moving scooter and killed his truck. Elmo got out and was going to try to stop the rascal with or without Bull's cooperation. When Elmo was almost to the rascal, Bull pulled over and put his head down on the handlebars of the rascal. "All right, Grandpa, your crime spree is over. I ought to kick your old, wrinkled ass for all the trouble you've got me into."

Just as Elmo reached for the kill switch on the rascal, the cane that Bull wielded like Excalibur came flying up from the blind side of the rascal. Again, Elmo went down, and everything got black for just a second. Old Mrs. Broxton had a six-foot-long nylon jump rope in the holding basket of her scooter, probably for some of the neighborhood kids that came to visit the rehab center. Bull grabbed the jump rope, hopped off the rascal with amazing speed, tied one end to Elmo's ankle, tied the other end to the back of the rascal, and started up again.

Elmo awakened to a lot of heat on his back and an extremely bumpy ride. He looked up into the sky and wondered for a moment if he was dead. Bull's laughter brought him back to reality. He raised his head enough to see that he was being pulled by the slow-moving rascal. He shouted threats and profanities at Bull to no avail. The asphalt was hot on his back, and his body was still taking a heck of a beating even though the rascal was moving so slow he could almost stand up. "Almost" being the key word.

Each time Elmo tried to stand up, the rascal would pick up a little speed, throwing him back down. By that time, Sheriff Duffie was on the scene, but, instead of intervening, he was just following and laughing so hard he almost wrecked his own car.

Bull finished off the whiskey and slammed the bottle down on the street, shattering it into lots of broken glass. Elmo was then dragged through the broken glass. Finally, the battery died on the rascal, and the terror was over. Judge Clayton pulled up right about that time and started damage control. He ordered Duffie to take his father home in the squad car as he took Elmo back to the El Camino.

"Go home and nurse your wounds, Elmo," said Judge Clayton. "Because you are still going to watch this old man for the rest of the week. Maybe now, you'll listen to me when I tell you he is dangerous."

Elmo took his two minor concussions, his tore-up back, and a heck of a story back home to tell Melvin. He was babysitting the devil, and it was a hell of a ride.

CHAPTER 15

Elmo came back and kept his end of the bargain he made with Judge Clayton. The rest of the week was fairly uneventful with the exceptions of a few more cruel statements and practical jokes made by Bull whenever the opportunity presented itself. The judge agreed that Friday would be Elmo's last day of watching Bull, so Elmo showed up in much better spirits that day. After breakfast, Bull asked Elmo if he could call his friend over to visit about their old war stories. Leroy Johnson was an old friend that had served in Germany with Bull. Elmo thought it would be a great idea to let Leroy come over and keep Bull occupied for the rest of the day.

While they were waiting on Leroy to arrive, Bull asked Elmo to take him for a walk out in the barnyard behind the house. Judge Clayton loved horses and had a beautiful two-story red barn behind the house. Elmo, hungry for fresh air, agreed and they walked out to the barn. It was a beautiful day with a slight breeze in the air, and the two men were soaking up the amazing weather. Bull apologized for his behavior throughout the week.

"I've got a little present to give you in appreciation and in apology," said Bull, laughing. "I know I can be a real pain in the rump to deal with, but I'm too old to change these stripes, I guess. Your gift is in the barn. Open the gate, and we'll get it."

Elmo was actually kind of excited at the prospect of a gift. In his life, he had not received many presents. As Elmo reached up to undo the latch on the big iron gate, Bull, with blazing speed, snapped a pair of handcuffs on Elmo's left wrist. The other end of the handcuffs he just as quickly snapped to the iron gate. Elmo was in shock. Everything had been so peaceful and quiet. They were getting along so well. Bull never said a word as Elmo shouted every terrible threat he could think of. He just turned around and headed for the house. Elmo was crushed at the thought of Bull going back to town to raise more hell. Judge Clayton would be so disappointed in him.

As if on cue, the pretty day started getting hot. After an hour or so, to Elmo's surprise, Bull and his friend Leroy walked out to the barnyard. They were holding a couple of cases that Elmo couldn't see very well. No matter how much he cursed and threatened, the two men ignored him completely as they were assembling something from the cases. The silence was unnerving. Ever so often, they would take a break and lean on the fence, just staring at Elmo and pushing their false teeth in and out with no hands. It was the strangest thing in the world to see those teeth go out and suck back in. Elmo felt like he was stuck in the middle of a bad dream, and he desperately wanted to wake up.

Finally, they were through with whatever they were working on. As they drew within about fifty feet or so,

Elmo's heart sank when he saw what they were holding. They had two high-dollar paintball guns and several large bottles of different-colored paintballs. Elmo screamed at, threatened, and cursed the old men for all they were worth, but it did no good. The old soldiers opened fire. The paintballs hurt terribly as they hit him from head to toe. It was like a thousand tiny baseball bats beating him relentlessly. He screamed and screamed, but that did not slow the marksmen down one little bit. The guns would shoot as fast as the men could pull the triggers. Elmo tried to dance around and make them miss, but old Nazi killers didn't miss too often. Elmo tried to climb the iron gate he was cuffed to, but there was no escape to be had.

When the old men were through with their opening volley, they got more creative. Bull and Leroy decided to teach Elmo to dance. As they shot around his feet over and over, Elmo put on a show Riverdance would have been proud of. The two old men then began to gamble on more specialized shots. They would bet different-colored medications, pornographic magazines, and boxes of stockpiled candy on whether they could hit an earlobe in five shots, hit a certain finger, or drill Elmo in the privates. Elmo eventually just turned his back and began to cry. Finally, the assault was over.

Elmo turned back around to see that the old men had gone back to the house. He looked at his paint-covered watch. It would be another three hours until Judge Clayton got home. The sun had really come out and was doing its job. Sweat poured into Elmo's eyes. He had to be careful when trying to wipe the sweat because the paint he was covered in would sting badly when it got in his eyes. He looked like a handcuffed rainbow as he leaned against the gate. It was just so hot. Hearing something behind him, he spun around to see Leroy and Bull bringing out a pitcher of lemonade. It looked so good, and he could hear the ice clinking in the pitcher as they got closer.

"Now I know it is hot out here, boy. This was a heck of a rough goodbye present, and I probably should not have done it. Get you a drink of lemonade while I dig the key out of my pocket for the handcuffs. No hard feelings, boy, I've had a great week with you here watching me. You make me feel young again. You ought to take the job on full time."

"The hell you say," whispered Elmo, his throat parched with thirst. "I'd rather rot in prison than spend another minute with you."

"You're right, boy, I deserve that," said Bull, motioning for Leroy to hand Elmo the pitcher of lemonade.

Elmo turned the pitcher up and drank deeply from the iced lemonade. Even as he was swallowing the lemonade, two things hit home at the same terrible instant. One was the laughter of two cruel, old veterans. The other realization that hit home was even more terrifying. It was not lemonade he had just swallowed.

CHAPTER 16

Judge Clayton felt terrible that poor Elmo's body was covered in bruises from the paintball attack. Probably hoping that he did not get sued, he gave Elmo five hundred dollars and released him from any more of the nightmarish responsibility of being Bull Clayton's caregiver. For a solid week, Elmo and Melvin just sat at home and licked their wounds. Elmo felt sorry for the poor Germans and Japanese that may have got in Bull's way during the great and terrible World War Two.

After a week, the two men decided it was time to get out of the house. They decided to eat at the Greasy Spoon Diner and then make another midnight bombing run on Sheriff Duffie's place. Everything went smoothly. All the previous bombing runs were paying interest and dividends like gangbusters. The smell was becoming a force to be reckoned with. They decided to hide their bombs in the attic since the walls were getting a little full. While up in the attic, they heard the sound of a key in the front door of Duffie's house. Fear froze the two men into almost instant paralysis. Elmo motioned for Melvin to kill his flashlight while he quietly closed the opening to the attic behind him. Luckily, they had hid the El Camino very well and out of sight. If they could remain calm and quiet, they might be able to wait out whoever had just come inside the house.

Sheriff Duffie, his brother Jack Duffie, and Peter Scott came into the house. "My God, Duffie, it smells like absolute shit in this house," said Peter Scott.

"Hey, shut up," replied Duffie. "I'm having weird problems with the plumbing. I've already spent a boat-load of money trying to get it fixed."

"Well, it isn't working. I would burn this place down and start over."

Sweat was pouring from Elmo and Melvin as they tried to remain perfectly still. Elmo's heart was beating so fast, he was afraid it sounded like a bass drum to the men downstairs.

"Let's just get this over with," said Jack Duffie.

Jack owned a bail bond company in Eltonberry, and his brother, the sheriff, made sure he stayed in business. Peter Scott owned and operated the most successful insurance business in Eltonberry.

Peter Scott was obviously in charge of the little meeting. He was a man that was used to being in charge, that much was obvious. "I know this is not a comfortable situation, but we are in deep trouble. We lost a ton of money in Reno. We covered those losses by borrowing money from the kind of people that do not take excuses. If we don't have that money paid back soon, I assure you we will go missing. The Russians don't care that you are a sheriff or about anything else. And don't forget that the vig is still running up on what we owe every minute of every day. It's a terrible place we are at, but we've got it to do. Jack, do you have anyone picked out yet?"

"Yes," replied Jack. "I've got a woman that will be perfect. I bonded her out about a month ago for passing some bad checks. She has a couple of minor drug arrests in her rearview mirror also. John can arrest her again on some trumped-up charge. If she goes back to jail for long at all, social services will have to place her three kids in the foster system, and she knows it. She is out of choices, and she has absolutely no family in her life except a sister that she hasn't talked to in years. Her parents are dead, her husband died in a car wreck two years ago, and she is also a recovering alcoholic. We're not going to find anyone else that checks this many boxes for us."

"Damn it, I do not like there being kids involved," said Sheriff Duffie. "This could get really messy before it's all over, and I don't intend to rot in a prison somewhere."

"No, it will not get messy if we handle our business like professionals. And how would you like to spend eternity at the bottom of a freaking hole out in a corn field or at the bottom of a lake with a concrete block chained to your leg? I've got a professional contractor lined up to light the fire and make it look like an accident," said Peter Scott. "Jack, you will take out a hundred thousand on each of the kids, and you will take out three hundred thousand on her. We can't put any more on them without triggering a more intense scrutiny from the insurance company that I would not be able to squash. That is two hundred thousand a piece for each of us once this is done. I'll make sure there is no investigation from my company. We will be able to pay back the money we owe the syndicate and have a nice chunk to hang onto for ourselves."

"I don't like this," said Jack. "If there is an investigation from the insurance company or the state police, I'm the one with my name on all the paperwork as beneficiary. Not to mention, I've got to get this woman to marry me. She can't stand me, and she made that clear when I tried to proposition her after bonding her out last month."

"Stop whining, I told you there will be no investigation. If there is, I know exactly whose hands to put a little cash in to make it all go away. This will not fail. As for marrying you, she isn't going to have a choice if she cares about those kids. When John mysteriously finds drugs in her trunk after a routine traffic stop, you two will have to make her understand that her options are very limited. Marry you or lose her kids to the foster system. You be really nice to her for about sixty days, and this will all be a memory we can forget. We're in too deep to turn back now, and you both know it," said Peter.

"John, arrest this little bitch soon, and make sure she calls Jack for her bail. Time is not on our side. If she makes a big fuss, make sure she understands those kids are going into a very crowded and very cruel foster home situation. Keep her isolated as much as possible. We don't want her sharing her problems with anyone. I'll have the insurance policies drawn up and waiting. Once you guys are married, we will have her sign the policies. She doesn't even have to understand what she is signing. We wait about sixty days or so, and the accident happens when we all have air-tight alibis."

"What about the guy setting the fire?" asked Sheriff Duffie. "If he ever talked, he could bring us all down."

"He cost a lot because he never talks. He is a professional that was recommended by other professionals. Now, let's get out of here. I can't stand this smell anymore. I'd be embarrassed to live this way, John."

"You go to hell," replied the sheriff. "Come on, I'll buy you both a beer, and we can talk it over some more."

Elmo and Melvin heard the door shut, and the three men were gone. They sat still for another five minutes just staring at each other. They knew they had just heard the voice of evil plan the death of a woman and her three children for money. Being in shock, they got out of the house and into some fresh air as fast as they could. A storm was brewing. Lightning lit up the sky in the distance as they made their way back to the El Camino. Neither man slept much that night.

CHAPTER 17

For about a week, neither Elmo nor Melvin talked about what they had overheard. The two men were out of their element when it came to being heroes or doing the right thing. Besides, they did not even know these people, so they certainly didn't owe them anything. It would be suicidal to go up against the sheriff, his cruel brother, and one of the most connected and important businessmen in the entire county. Elmo insisted they probably were just talking trash anyway and trying to impress each other. Both men knew that was not the case.

Finally, they could not take it anymore. They stood up and went for a drive. They just happened to drive down the lonely country road that Rebecca Sanders and her three children lived on. Later in the day, Elmo and Melvin made a few phone calls and found out that Rebecca was arrested earlier in the week by Sheriff John Duffie and given bail that very night by Jack Duffie. The house was in terrible shape. They didn't know what they were doing as they pulled up in the driveway.

A small girl no older than seven was pushing a toddler on a swing set that had seen much better days. Another little guy was making mud pies as Elmo and Melvin walked up in the yard. "Hello, there," said Elmo, smiling. "How are you guys doing today?"

The kids said nothing. Elmo could see in their eyes something familiar. He knew what it meant to grow up hurting. Suddenly, the screen door opened, and Rebecca Sanders walked out onto the old wooden porch. She had a black eye, and her lip was swollen where she had taken a beating in the not-too-distant past. Past all the bruises, it was obvious she was a pretty lady that had lived a very hard life. Elmo knew that for every bruise a woman endured on the outside, there were countless more on the inside. He had seen more than his fair share of abuse growing up. The world was just too full of bruises.

"Can I help you with something, sir?" asked Rebecca.

"No, ma'am, I don't guess so. I'm new to the area, and I was just wondering if there were any houses for rent out this way. I was just looking around. I didn't realize this one was occupied."

"Well, this is a rental house. We are going to be moving into my fiancé's place in about a month. He is doing some remodeling, so he wanted us to stay here in the meantime. I'm sure you could rent this old place if you were interested. It could use some fixing up. Mr. Johnson, from Franklin street, is the owner of the house."

"Well, thank you, ma'am. I'll take it under consideration. If it's not too forward, may I ask who you are marrying?"

"I will be marrying Jack Duffie," said Rebecca, a hollowness to her voice and a look of sadness on her face.

"Well, congratulations, and I wish you all the best. Thank you for your time."

Elmo and Melvin had a meeting that night. They wanted to help the nice lady and her children, but they knew it was impossible. Whatever was in motion had nothing to do with them. This was too big to stop, and they could not go to the authorities under any circumstances. Who would believe a couple of rascals like them over the likes of John Duffie and Peter Scott? If the Duffie brothers and Peter Scott were willing to kill this woman and her children for money, they would not hesitate to make Elmo and Melvin disappear. No, the safe play was to put this out of their minds and go on living. Being in that attic was terrible luck, but the decision was made to stay out of it. The meeting was adjourned. Elmo and Melvin each went to bed with heavy hearts that night. Elmo tossed and turned, but sleep would not come. Every time he closed his eyes, he could see the faces of those three little children, and he could see the pretty face of a woman that had probably had a real pitiful hand dealt to her in this life.

Another thunderstorm had let loose outside, and each time the lightning lit up the sky, it would throw eerie shadows across the wall of Elmo's room. The shadows looked like flames. Elmo finally gave up on sleeping and went to get a glass of milk. Melvin was sitting on the couch and staring at the wall.

"You couldn't sleep either, huh?" asked Melvin.

"I guess I can't," replied Elmo, walking over to the window and staring outside at the wind and rain. "Melvin, do you think there really is a God and all that jazz? I mean if there was a God, I suppose that would mean there had to be a devil too."

"I don't know, Elmo. I'd like to think there is a God up there, but you and I are probably in big trouble if there is."

"Yes, I expect you are right about that, Melvin. I've done lots of wrong in my life. If there was a devil, I bet he is mighty happy at the thought of what is going to happen to those three little kids."

"Yes, I'm sure he would love the Duffie brothers," replied Melvin.

"If there is a God, he ought to be the one saving this family. That's what he gets paid the big bucks for, isn't it? I guess he's not too worried about this family, or he would send someone to help them," said Elmo.

"But what if it wasn't an accident we were in that attic when they had that little meeting? What if God did send someone, and it was us?"

"Yeah, right, Melvin, I don't think so. God could have the FBI or even Delta Force intervene for this family if He was really worried about them. I seriously doubt He had two rascals like us destined to hide turd bags in the sheriff's house so we could hear about this family. It sounds kind of crazy when you even say it, doesn't it?"

"I guess so, Elmo," admitted Melvin.

The storm was picking up in intensity, and it made a whistling sound as it blew through the old oak tree in their front yard. Both men were quiet as they listened to the old shack moan and rattle under the strength of the wind. "Melvin, where is the black book we always keep score in for dealing with people?"

"It's on the coffee table."

Elmo walked over and picked up the old black book. He sat down on the other side of the couch from Melvin and started flipping through the old, tattered pages full of names and check marks. Neither man spoke. The rain on the tin roof sang a time-honored song as the boys remained quiet. Finally, Elmo took a deep breath and tossed the book over to Melvin.

"Put the devil's name down and a check mark by it. I think the devil must be a huge horse's ass. What do you say we kick him in his damn teeth and help this family out of this situation?" asked Elmo.

"I thought you would never ask," said Melvin, smiling. "I'm your right-hand man."

"Good," replied Elmo. "Meeting adjourned."

CHAPTER 18

E lmo and Melvin had finally drifted off to sleep, each with a thousand different questions dancing around in their heads. The first and best question either of them could come up with consisted of what to do first. Over breakfast, it was decided that they definitely needed some help. Neither had a very long list of people in life they could call on for help. As a matter of fact, the boys had to admit the list was just about non-existent. They considered Judge Clayton, but what if he simply called Sheriff Duffie on the matter, believing it to be a misunderstanding? Duffie would not hesitate to kill them both. They finally decided their only option was family.

Melvin had no family, and Elmo had very little. Elmo had a cousin that went by the name of Squirrel Bogg. He lived in the hill country. You would have to be lost on top of lost to find how far back in the woods Squirrel and his family lived. Their small community was a throwback to bygone times. Elmo wasn't even sure if he could get ahold of them. Elmo's mother was not exactly the most loved member of the family, so Elmo was worried they would tell him to get lost.

Finally getting his nerve up, Elmo placed the call and asked Squirrel for his help. He didn't even have to explain the situation. Squirrel did not hesitate even in the slightest. Squirrel told them he could catch a ride as far as the nearest bus stop. He would take the bus to Fullerton, and Elmo could pick him up from there the following morning.

"Now, Melvin, Squirrel is the big warrior type. He is exactly the kind of person we need on our team to help us deal with this situation, but he has also got a few problems."

"What kind of problems?"

"Well, the kind between the ears. He is not quite right mentally at times, or at least he wasn't as a kid. I haven't seen him since we were kids, you understand. He is probably just as normal as we are now."

Elmo was trying to slowly prepare his buddy, because Melvin had endured a life-long fear of crazy people that had followed him all his life. It could have been because his own mother was a loon, or it could have been for no reason at all. Melvin's nerves were bad on a good and calm day, but when around someone that came across as touched or crazy, Melvin's left leg began to bounce and shake like there was an earthquake going on inside it. He wouldn't even wash the El Camino at Crazy Suds car wash or go to Crazy Al's furniture liquidation sales. It was obvious Melvin was doubting the wisdom of bringing Squirrel into the situation. Elmo explained that it could not be helped. Squirrel was a big boy, he was fearless, and he was a fighter. There was no way they would be able to defeat the Duffie boys without help.

The next day, Elmo and Melvin rolled up beside a little sandwich shop beside the bus stop in Fullerton. Melvin was very nervous as they looked around. He got even more nervous as Squirrel came lumbering out of the sandwich shop. He was every bit of six feet and four inches in his sock feet. He would weigh in at a good three hundred pounds or close to it. Somehow the large size and girth did not equate to muscles or toughness, though. He just kind of looked like a big, chubby teddy bear. Now, an El Camino has no backseat, which meant three men, one of them very large, were going to have an extremely tight ride back to Eltonberry. Before Melvin could jump out and get in the back of the El Camino, Squirrel had already crammed himself into the car. With Elmo driving, that left Melvin stuffed in the middle with barely enough room to breathe. Elmo stopped at a drive-through on the way out of Fullerton to get everyone a soda, but Squirrel said he wasn't thirsty.

Now Squirrel sure wasn't shy or quiet. He was as friendly as could be and talked like they were all long lost brothers. He kept trying to hug Elmo in the driver's seat, which meant poor Melvin was getting seriously squeezed between the two each time Squirrel needed more affection. Melvin hated being in the middle almost as much as he hated crazy people. It made Melvin beyond uncomfortable that Squirrel kept putting his arm around him. When Squirrel undid his belt and then unbuttoned his pants to get more comfortable for the long ride, Melvin's tension meter went up a few more notches. Every mile or so, Squirrel, who was not thirsty only a few minutes earlier, would reach over and take a big sip out of Melvin's soda. Melvin didn't do well with the thought of germs, and he decided to gift his soda to their new visitor. Elmo and his cousin caught up on old times as the miles went by. The boys filled Squirrel in on the entire situation they were facing with the Duffie Brothers and Peter Scott. Soon they were almost home, and Elmo made a proclamation.

"Boys, we are about to go to war together. They say there is no bond as tight as the one made in combat. I think it would be a good idea if we confessed something very personal to each other that no one else would know about us. I believe that would bring us closer together and make a bond that could prove important when the chips are on the table. I'll go first."

Elmo confessed to the others about a terrible crush he used to have on one of his teachers in high school, and that he had her initials tattooed in very small letters on the back of one of his shoulders. Melvin confessed that he'd had a bed wetting problem as a child that sometimes still reared its ugly head. The problem was most prevalent during stormy weather.

It was Squirrel's turn, and it grew deathly silent as the big man cleared his throat. It was obvious he was about to let go of something that was very delicate. You could have heard a pin drop in that El Camino.

"I had some children that didn't make it," said Squirrel, tears starting to roll down his face.

"My God, Squirrel, I had no idea. You don't have to go any further with that if you don't want to."

"No, it's okay, I think it would be good for me to get this said and out in the open. When I was a young boy hitting that puberty age we all hit, my dad brought home a big, fine hog. It was my responsibility to feed her and keep her clean. Every day I cleaned her pen and bathed her. I spent countless hours bathing that hog. She would get so dirty each day, and I just had to scrub her and scrub her. She kept staring at me more and more...my God, that hog stared right into the soul of me, boys. I will never forget the color of her eyes as long as I live. Well, later that year, she had a litter of little ones that looked…"

Squirrel burst into full-blown sobbing. Melvin gasped for air, realizing he had not breathed for about a minute or so. Big tears were rolling down Squirrel's cheeks. Through the sobbing, Squirrel tried to finish. "Those little fellas looked just like me. Daddy was embarrassed. He made us eat every one of those poor little bastards that winter. Daddy was worried what the neighbors might say, damn his hide. To this day, I can't eat a bacon sandwich without breaking down into tears." Squirrel was sobbing uncontrollably and banging his fist against the dash.

Elmo and Melvin sat frozen and staring forward, their eyes not even capable of blinking. The only sound in the car was the manic bouncing of Melvin's left leg. Soon they were home, and, once inside, Melvin took Elmo into the bathroom and locked the door.

"He has got to go, Elmo," whispered Melvin. "If I'm not mistaken, I believe we just heard that man describe getting intimate with a pig, having little pig babies that looked like him, and then eating their asses. This man will kill us in our sleep, I am begging you to get rid of him."

"No, we can't do it. We need him, Melvin, and you know it. Look how big he is. He will be a big help if this thing gets physical with the Duffies, and it probably will. As long as it doesn't storm tonight, you can bunk with me, and we will give him your bed. Stay the course, Melvin, stay the course."

After supper, the men decided to turn in early. As Elmo and Melvin lay in the bed they now had to share, they could hear it begin to lightly rain on the old tin roof.

"Melvin, you better not piss in this bed tonight."

CHAPTER 19

Allie Sanders looked at the clock. She knew the man that had invaded their world would be coming by soon. Jack Duffie had called earlier to let Rebecca know he would be by later that night. She hated Jack because he was always so cruel to her mother. Her mother had warned her to always stay locked in her room with her little brothers no matter what they heard. Jack was always drunk, it seemed, and he would say such horrible things to her mother. Some nights he would hit her mother over and over. He was always threatening to have her sent back to jail if she did not marry him. Allie was afraid it was only a matter of time before he came into their room and started beating her and her little brothers. Her greatest fear was that Jack would either kill her mother or have her sent back to prison. Allie didn't know what would happen to them if her mom was gone.

Life had not been easy for the Sanders family. She missed her dad a lot, since the car accident took him away.

Her mom had made a lot of mistakes, but Allie knew her mother loved her. Her mom had also really been trying to get her life straight, and then, earlier in the week, she was arrested for no good reason at all. They were on their way back from the grocery store when they were pulled over by the sheriff. The sheriff claimed to smell drugs in their car, and then he mysteriously found a small bag of white powder in their trunk. Allie was young, but she knew something was not right. Her mom had cried all week long at the thought of having to marry her disgusting probation officer or lose her children.

Allie heard Jack's truck pull up in the yard. She looked over at her little brothers sleeping. They needed diapers badly, but there was no money. Her mom's job had played out almost a week ago, and then came the arrest. Allie could tell by the sound of Jack's heavy footsteps that he was very drunk. It wasn't long before she could hear him threatening her mother. In short order, the beating started. It was getting harder and harder to pray. She buried her head under the pillow and asked God to send an angel to save her mother and her brothers. Once again, no angel would show up that night at the Sanders home.

Rebecca had no more strength left. The beating was the worst one yet. She hated this man with a passion. She was no great catch, and she knew it. Why was he so determined to marry her? When he was too tired to throw her around the room anymore, Jack Duffie gave her two choices. Either she signed the marriage papers the next morning or he was going to give her next beating to the children. He convinced her that it had nothing to do with actual marriage or romance. He was set to inherit a lot of money, but the will would only pay out if he was a married man. It was just a formality, and they could get the marriage annulled soon after. He even promised to give her a few thousand dollars after the annulment so she could do better for her family. Rebecca was so tired, but she would do anything to avoid going back to prison and losing her children. She signed the paperwork before the justice of the peace the next morning. It broke her heart, but, on paper, she was now a married woman.

CHAPTER 20

Elmo, Melvin, and Squirrel spent all morning going over their options. The men were at a real loss for what to do next. They could not warn the Sanders family because Rebecca couldn't protest or flee without running afoul of the law, losing her children, and going back to jail. They couldn't go to Judge Clayton because he would simply write them off or call Sheriff Duffie, which would certainly get people killed. Sheriff Duffie and Peter Scott were very connected men in the state, and there was no way to know how far or wide those connections went.

After brainstorming for a while, Squirrel suggested they go do some exercises in the backyard to try and tone up for the upcoming showdown. Squirrel went to change clothes, and Elmo and Melvin went outside and began to stretch. When Squirrel finally stepped out the back door, the boys could not believe their own eyes. Squirrel was wearing nothing but a super tight pair of zebra print spandex shorts, some cowboy boots, and a pair of dark sunglasses. His belly was huge, and his breasts were not far behind his belly. The muffin tops and love handles were stuff for the record books.

As he began to do jumping jacks, Elmo had to look away. Melvin was pretty much just working out his left leg at this point. There was something unseemly about those bouncing breasts. Melvin was visibly shaking, but he could not take his eyes off Squirrel's bouncing boobs. After about eight jumping jacks, Squirrel was gassed. He immediately insisted they move from exercise to combat training. "Melvin, I want you to hit me in the stomach just as hard as you can. Don't hold anything back," said Squirrel, bracing his stomach as tight as he could.

"No, I'm not going to hit you in the stomach," replied Melvin.

"Do it!" shouted Squirrel, bracing himself again. "Do it now!"

"No, I will not do it."

"So help me God, if you don't hit me in the stomach within one minute, I will kiss you right on your mouth!"

Almost quicker than the human eye could see, Melvin had wound up all the strength his little body had and hit Squirrel right in the belly. Melvin hit him with all the intensity of a man that really didn't want to be kissed. The blow came so quickly that Squirrel did not have time to brace himself. His face turned a nasty shade of crimson red as he fell to his knees, gasping for air that was not there. Squirrel then fell over and began to roll on the ground. Unfortunately, he ended up rolling on top of a fire ant mound. Within seconds, he was covered in ants.

Elmo and Melvin panicked and began trying to slap the ants off Squirrel's big body to no avail. They then went for the water hose, but, by that time, Squirrel had ripped those spandex shorts off and took off at a full-blown sprint down the road. He was screaming like a madman, and fat was flapping in every direction. He eventually reached Mrs. Norris' yard, just as naked as the day God placed him on this earth. Mrs. Norris was Elmo's closest neighbor, and she was always on the lookout for sexual predators. She called the police station seven or eight times a month with suspicions about different people in town. She once called 911 because a man, while filling his car up at the gas station, looked at her while he was inserting the gas nozzle into his tank. Another time, Mrs. Norris called the law on the elderly gentleman that ran the local dog shelter, because she looked out her window and saw two dogs engaged in an intimate act. She was positively convinced that the old gent had trained those two dogs to come to her yard and "send her a message."

When Squirrel came running down her driveway, scratching at his own flesh, screaming at the top of his lungs, and body parts jiggling and shaking like some kind of drunken tornado, Mrs. Norris was more than ready. She grabbed her twelve-gauge shotgun and emptied it in his direction. Luckily, there was nothing in it but old rock salt her deceased husband had stockpiled for trespassing teenagers. It hurt like the dickens as it tore into his flesh, but it made him forget all about the ants. Mrs. Norris knew she could not see well and had probably missed him, so she ran out into the yard and unchained her pit bull, Brutus.

"Get the pervert, Brutus, get him!"

Brutus must have hated sex offenders as much as Mrs. Norris because he had Squirrel's ass in his sights and was closing in quick. Right before Brutus brought a tragic end to the day for Squirrel, Elmo came flying over the hill in the El Camino, pulling up alongside the naked Squirrel. Squirrel jumped in the back, and the would-be sex offender drove off and out of Mrs. Norris' life forever.

CHAPTER 21

Officer Hillshire had taken law enforcement as far as he could, but he could not go any farther. His condition was just too out of control. He saw germs around every corner. Each time he seemed to be on the verge of a breakthrough, he would run into a situation that crushed him. He was already on thin ice when old Bull Clayton spit on him. The ice broke as he wrecked his police cruiser into that telephone pole.

Luckily, an old friend had been able to get him a job at Eltonberry's only hospital. It was not a huge facility, but it consisted of three floors and about sixty-five rooms. He had been able to get work on the third floor where patients went as they were in recovery. It did not pay much, but it was work. His job was that of an orderly, and he worked under a very strict head nurse that demanded a level of cleanliness almost impossible for her employees to comply with.

The job was absolutely perfect for John Hillshire. He was actually getting to work at destroying germs and getting paid for it. Nurse Betty Giles was blown away at just how clean John was able to keep his section of the hospital. John was able to keep his own working environment totally germless, and instead of being treated as an oddball, he was celebrated as very efficient.

It had been several days since Squirrel Bogg's encounter with Mrs. Norris. Squirrel had tried to recover from his terrible day of rock salt and ants the best he could. The ant bites were terrible and had caused a lot of pain. His torso and back had been chewed on pretty good by the ants, and his backside took a good dose of Mrs. Norris' rock salt. Overall, Squirrel felt pretty lucky that Brutus had not caught up with him.

Elmo had given him some ointment he found in the medicine cabinet that helped with the ant bites. Squirrel had a mean reaction to the bites, causing him to scratch all the time unless he had the ointment on. The tube was almost empty, so Squirrel told Elmo he wanted to look around town and pick up some more ointment and a few other things. Melvin prayed one of the things he picked up would be deodorant. Elmo dropped him off in Eltonberry and told him to be outside one of the thrift shops in a few hours. After looking around for an hour or so, Squirrel decided that Eltonberry did not have much to offer a fellow looking to explore. He browsed through the few department stores and flea markets in town and finally wandered into the hospital to see about getting some more ointment for his ant bites.

He was delighted to see that the hospital had an elevator. Being from the hills, he had never ridden on an elevator, and it was high adventure. It was a very short ride considering the hospital only had three floors, but there was no limit on how many times a man could ride. It did not even require tickets for the ride. Squirrel loved the feeling he got in his belly as the elevator started and stopped.

It was lunchtime and John Hillshire was going to splurge and go to a particularly clean little diner not far from the hospital. He was making progress one step at a time. When the elevator opened on the third floor, Mr. Hillshire was perturbed to see someone already inside it. He started to take the stairs, but he decided this could be therapeutic for him. Stepping inside the elevator, he stared at Squirrel Bogg and wondered who the stranger was.

The elevator started back down toward the first floor, but it very suddenly slammed to a stop. The stop was so abrupt that Mr. Hillshire and Squirrel were both thrown off their feet. Panic immediately set in for John Hillshire. He did not feel panicked because the elevator was stuck, he felt panicked because he was breathing the same air as the big stranger in a very confined space. Being the first time he had ever ridden in an elevator, Squirrel assumed it might be something that happened at regular intervals.

John grabbed the emergency phone, and the lady working the front desk informed him that the elevator was stuck for no apparent reason at all. The elevator was ancient, just like the building it was in. Hospital management had called a crew from a neighboring town that was proficient at working on elevators of all types and ages. It would be some time before the crew would be able to make it there. The lady began to read from a script, warning all those trapped inside not to panic. She also informed Mr. Hillshire that he would not be paid for the time spent "resting" in the elevator.

Squirrel introduced himself to John Hillshire and tried to shake his hand. John politely waved off the handshake. He was convinced he could see spit flying out of Squirrel's mouth with each word spoken.

"Mr. Squirrel, it is nice to meet you, but I really am not in the mood for talking. Let's conserve our energy and just wait quietly for help if you don't mind. I mean no offense."

"None taken, guy, I totally agree. I can't stand someone that runs off at the mouth all the time, and—" Squirrel farted without trying to. He had eaten red beans and rice for lunch in town, and the beans had upset his stomach. "Excuse me, sir, that one slipped out."

Mr. Hillshire was mortified. He felt as if the floor had just opened up beneath him. He started to go into meltdown mode, but he caught himself and went to a happy place in his mind, instead. John Hillshire's happy place was extremely clean and not crowded at all. He took a deep breath and addressed Squirrel in the calmest voice he could muster. "Mister, I am going to have to ask you not to pass wind in this elevator again under any circumstances."

"I can't make you any promises, guy, I just had a big bowl of—" Squirrel farted again. "Damn it, I'm sorry, guy, I really do apologize. This could get a little ugly, I'm afraid, since my stomach is feeling a tad bit funny." Squirrel put on some chapstick, and he offered John some after he was through with it.

Hillshire was starting to crack up. He slid down the side of the elevator wall and just put his head in his hands. He begged God to do a miracle and make the elevator start moving again. He then begged God for another miracle—that He would keep the big stranger from farting, spitting, or sharing any germs of any kind. God answered neither prayer.

When Mr. Hillshire looked up again, he immediately wanted to die. Squirrel had his pants all the way down around his ankles and was attempting to urinate in his plastic soda bottle. Hillshire could see splatter and screamed out a terrible shriek from somewhere deep within. The loud shriek made Squirrel jump, only producing more splatter and spillage.

"What in God's name are you doing, you fool?!" shouted Hillshire, almost in tears.

"I had a Slurpee an hour ago, and I just finished drinking this soda. I had to go. Why are you getting so excited?"

"I have a very real and very terrible problem with germs, bodily functions, and close contact with other human beings. I am begging you to stop your 'functions' and just stay on your side of the darn elevator. Please make sure the lid to that soda is screwed on very freaking tight too," begged Hillshire.

Squirrel could not stop talking. He was a friendly sort and loved to talk whenever he could get someone to listen. He now had a captive audience. He talked of his childhood, his past loves, his devil hunting adventures, his cousin Elmo, and every other thing that happened to cross his mind. Every few minutes, he would pass wind again as he talked. John could feel sweat breaking out all over his body as he tried to ignore the nightmares of the elevator. The smell was starting to get worse, which made John's anxiety reach new levels as Squirrel continued to chatter on and on.

Squirrel especially focused on his devil hunting escapades back in the hills. The stories never slowed down. He was like a chain smoker. As one story came to an end, he was immediately starting another. He demanded that Hillshire rack his brain and try to give him any leads on suspected devils in the local area. After being badgered for information for so long, he couldn't take it anymore. He promised Squirrel he would give him a hot lead on a suspected devil in the area if he would just shut up for a little while after the information was given. Squirrel agreed, and John just said the first thing that popped into his mind. "The devil has been seen in our town in a green suit with two gold teeth and a slight limp. Now, a deal is a deal, you be quiet and rest for a bit," pleaded John.

Squirrel had trouble keeping his end of the bargain and wanted to discuss the time he caught the mange from sleeping with an orphaned dog he found in the hills while hunting. Thinking about those memories always made Squirrel itch all over. He began to scratch his head, sending dandruff in an array of directions. Next, the ant bites started itching, and he started scratching them desperately. He decided the shirt had to go next, as it was irritating his skin. John was finding it difficult to swallow, and it was even getting tough to breathe. As he looked at the now shirtless Squirrel covered in red bumps all over, he could feel his fingers starting to slip from the mental ledge he was hanging from. Squirrel suddenly got quiet and started looking around, as if perplexed.

"What are you looking for?" demanded Hillshire.

"Well, I really need to do number two, but I don't think I can get it into that soda bottle without making a hell of a mess," said Squirrel, serious as a heart attack. "At least, I couldn't do it without help."

"No, don't do that!" shouted Hillshire, jumping to his feet. "I'll give you one hundred dollars not to even consider doing that."

Squirrel was holding his stomach and grimacing. "I'll take the money, but I may end up having to give you a refund. Those beans have really roughed me up." For a few moments all was quiet in the elevator except for Squirrel's rumbling belly and the great drumbeat of John Hillshire's terrified heart.

"You know we may not make it out of this alive," said Squirrel. I'm sitting here and thinking back over my life. I still had a lot of living left to do, but I had some good times too. I'll never forget the first time I drove a truck, the first time I killed a deer, and the first time I ever saw a woman naked."

Hillshire lifted his head up. "If you insist on talking, you have finally hit on something that could be interesting. Let's hear about the first time you ever saw a naked woman."

"Well, it was a hot July day—you know, a real scorcher. I had been mowing grass and went in the house to get some lemonade. Hearing something in the bathroom, I opened the door and walked inside. She was just laying there in the tub, smoking a cigarette. I just stood there and stared at her with this warm feeling washing all over me."

"Yes, what happened next?" asked Hillshire, finally interested in one of Squirrel's stories.

"Then Momma told me to get the hell out of the bathroom, or she was going to call Daddy at work."

"Damn it, man, that is disgusting. You have got serious issues. You really sent that story to hell in a handbag. Let's go back to not talking at all."

Squirrel managed to stay quiet for almost five minutes, and then the talking started up again. "If I don't make it, guy, I want you to know that you have got my blessing to go ahead and eat me. I only ask that you would not eat my face or any of my privy parts."

"What in the heck are you talking about? We have only been in here for an hour or so. They should be here any minute. Something is wrong with you, guy, if you are already thinking about eating another human being," said Hillshire, disgusted.

"I don't think anyone is coming at all. They are probably bricking us in as we speak. They told us about the 'rescue' to shut us up and keep us calm, and I was giving you permission to eat me, Mr. Ungrateful. But I would like your blessing to eat you, also, if you should pass first."

"You go to hell," replied Hillshire.

Hillshire and Squirrel both eventually dozed off. After about twenty minutes, Squirrel woke up and noticed Hillshire was unconscious and not moving. He went over and examined the motionless man for a moment. He put his hand under Hillshire's nose to see if he could feel breath. Squirrel stared at his chest, but he felt like he could see no rising and falling. Not noticing any obvious signs of life, he was thankful he had planned ahead. He took out his little folding knife and examined Hillshire's body for a while. After asking God to forgive him, he finally decided on a wing. Squirrel was nervous, but he went ahead and made a small slice on Hillshire's arm.

John Hillshire jumped up in time to see the shirtless and sweating Squirrel kneeling over him with a tiny pocketknife open with blood on the end of it. Seeing his arm had a small cut on it, he began to scream uncontrollably.

Squirrel was scared and jumped back over to his side of the elevator. Hillshire was on the emergency phone using profanities to no avail. "Margaret, I know where you live, and I will burn your freaking house down if you don't get this elevator moving right now!" Hillshire began to beat his fist against the side of the elevator, and then he tried to climb up the side of the elevator and get through one of the ceiling panels to no avail.

"Guy, calm down, please," said Squirrel very calmly. "Now that was my bad. I thought you had crossed on over river death, and I was just trying to survive the best way I knew how."

"You haven't been in this elevator but a few hours, you imbecile! You already said you had beans for lunch. It is only three-thirty in the afternoon, and you are so worried about starving that you start carving on my ass. I'm going to kill you. I swear I'm going to kill you if—"

The elevator, without warning, whirred back to life and started moving again. When it got to the bottom floor and the doors opened, John Hillshire started running. He ran and ran. No one in the town of Eltonberry ever saw John Hillshire again. It was rumored that he developed a patent on a new cleaning solvent and became a very rich man. It was also rumored that he lost his mind and ended up in a mental institution out west.

Elmo picked up Squirrel about thirty minutes later. "How was your day, Squirrel?"

"It was good. I think I made a new friend."

CHAPTER 22

Squirrel seemed to slide in and out of different worlds easily. Twice, Elmo and Melvin caught him talking on an imaginary phone that wasn't really there. Once, Melvin had walked in the kitchen while Squirrel was having a very heated argument with a box of cereal. Melvin locked himself in the bathroom for half the morning after that episode. They had all been locked down in the shack for days while they brainstormed, and they were starting to get stir crazy, so they decided to do something about it.

The three men agreed they needed to get out of the house for a few hours, so they planned a trip to the Dark Horse Lounge. Pretty women and alcohol always seemed to make one's problems seem smaller for a few hours. The Dark Horse was considered Eltonberry's closest thing to cutting edge. Cutting edge in Eltonberry just meant no one threw peanut shells on the floor. Elmo and Melvin did not voice it out loud, but they were a little embarrassed by just how tight Squirrel's jeans were. He called them his "female bait." The tight jeans and healthy love handles gave new meaning to the term "muffin top."

As they walked into the bar, it was apparent it would not be an ordinary night. Squirrel, without hesitation, walked up to the most beautiful woman in the bar, who happened to be sitting at a table with her boyfriend. Squirrel just stared at the woman for a good minute until it was getting very uncomfortable. It got even more uncomfortable when he opened his mouth. "You've got a decision to make tonight, ma'am. You can go home with this feller, and nine months from tonight, you can have a mangy, flea-bitten, half-dead mule limp out of your uterus. That is option one. Option two is you can go home with me tonight, and nine months from tonight, you can have a great big American stud come charging out of you in all the glory of the heavens. It's your call, think it over. I'll be at the bar."

The woman's face was frozen in some kind of strange terror as Squirrel turned and walked away. Her boyfriend was beside himself with rage and being held back by a couple of friends. Elmo and Melvin were just in shock. They could barely manage to make eye contact with an attractive woman, much less make a proposition like that.

Squirrel then walked up to the bar and ordered a glass of warm milk with seven drops of hot sauce and a human hair in it. The bartender tried to laugh it off, but Squirrel grabbed him by the shirt and demanded the drink again. Finally, the manager okayed the order, and Squirrel got his warm milk, hot sauce, and human hair. He downed it without taking a breath.

For a while, Squirrel was all right. He kept downing the drink he referred to as the "cat killer," and if the bartender deviated on the number of hot sauce drops or the human hair, Squirrel knew it. It was almost as if he was getting drunk, but there was no alcohol in the drink. Soon he was out on the dance floor doing things that hill people referred to as dancing. Just looking at it, a man would have to describe it as some strange form of stationary skiing. At first, everyone just stopped their own dancing and stared in disbelief, but, to Elmo and Melvin's utter shock, soon everyone in the bar was doing Squirrel's dance. Even more amazing, the beautiful woman he had hit on earlier had come over and started doing the dance one on one with Squirrel. Elmo would not have believed this story had he not seen it unfold right before his eyes.

The music was loud, and the bass was pumping. Everyone seemed to be having a good time. Suddenly, Big Sue walked in the door, walked over to a table, and had a seat. She had certainly lost no weight since her brief employment with Elmo's massage parlor and cathouse. Her complexion had cleared up a little, which still did not help the final product very much. The very instant Squirrel saw her, the room froze in time for him. He pushed past the beautiful young woman trying to dance with him, and he walked right up to Sue's table. Big Sue had just ordered two dozen buffalo wings and a pitcher of beer.

"Ma'am, you are about the finest thing I've ever laid my eyes on. I have every intention of making you my wife and living out the rest of my days staring into your eyes."

"Screw you," replied Big Sue, leaning back in her chair and belching.

"My name is Squirrel Bogg. Take a good look at me, your children will look just like me."

Big Sue was starting to get agitated. "Take a walk, or you are about to wish you had. I'm in no mood for your joking, mister."

Squirrel kneeled down and tried to kiss her hand. Big Sue moved as quick as a cat, and, before anyone could respond, she had whipped out a pair of brass knuckles and hit Squirrel right upside his head. Squirrel didn't wake up until he was in the El Camino and halfway home. Elmo and Melvin tried to explain the fact that she had been a prostitute in their cathouse, but Squirrel got so mad he almost made Elmo wreck the car.

"She's my baby kitten," whined Squirrel, his voice tender, and his heart sick with love.

"If that's a baby kitten, I'd hate like hell to see the momma cat," said Elmo.

CHAPTER 23

The next morning, Elmo got up extra early and decided to make breakfast for his two buddies. As he stood over the stove and tended the eggs, Elmo's mind kept going back to the sight of Rebecca Sanders as she walked out on her porch. Her face beaten and yet still beautiful. He felt a growing rage inside of him for Jack Duffie. Any man that would hit a woman was a coward in Elmo's opinion. The three trashy jerks were forcing Rebecca into an unwanted marriage if she wanted her family to stay together, and, on top of all that, they only wanted the marriage to take place so they could burn up the entire family for insurance money. Elmo felt something happen inside his heart the day she came out on her porch. He wasn't sure what exactly it was he had felt that day, but it was something that would not go away.

His two roommates got up and came to breakfast. They were recounting their exploits from the night before and trying to enjoy the morning. Everything seemed fine, but as Melvin put the first bite of eggs in his mouth, Squirrel flipped out. He screamed, jumped out of his own chair, and grabbed Melvin from behind. He was trying to do an awkward Heimlich maneuver on him and screaming for him to spit out the egg. Finally, the egg came up, and Squirrel calmed down. Poor Melvin was terrified and confused.

"My God have mercy on us all. Melvin, do you know what you almost did, boy? We had not said grace yet."

"You've got to be kidding me!" shouted Melvin in disbelief.

"Melvin, if you would have swallowed that piece of food without saying grace, do you understand what would have happened? The devil himself would have come into your room tonight at the midnight hour, peeled your skin from your body with his razor-sharp hayfork, and worn your skin as a coat for all eternity," said Squirrel, in absolute sincerity. "Didn't your momma ever teach you these things? Didn't you ever go to Sunday School?"

Elmo and Melvin were in disbelief. They just simply stared at each other in shock. Squirrel, without warning, reached out and grabbed both their hands and began to pray, "Dear God, I ask you to bless this fine meal that Cousin Elmo has prepared this morning. God, I also ask you to forgive Melvin for the filthy magazines I found under his bed last night and for the strange stains on his sheets. Amen, let's eat, boys!"

Melvin had lost his appetite and kind of stumbled to the bathroom, locking the door behind him. Elmo finished breakfast and straightened up the house for a while. That evening, he announced that he and Melvin were going out for some groceries. He told Squirrel to just stay home and relax, because he knew that Melvin desperately needed a break from being around Squirrel. Elmo noticed the trick or treaters just starting to come out as he and Melvin took off for the grocery store. Halloween had really snuck up on them this year. Most of the kids were all dressed in the same devil costume, because one of the local retailers was running an awesome sale on the overstocked costume. Elmo had forgotten all about it being Halloween. He just had too much on his mind these days.

Now, in the mountains, there was no such thing as Halloween. The devil was taken very seriously and would never have been celebrated. It had just turned dark outside, and Squirrel was laying on the couch watching a western when the doorbell rang. Squirrel got up and went to answer the door. As he looked through the peephole, he grabbed his heart and felt frozen in terror. His mother had always told him that the devil would come for him one day. That day was here. Outside Elmo's little shack stood no less than seven horned devils, a small hairy gorilla, and a fairy princess of some kind or another. They were somewhat smaller than he had always anticipated, but that was trivial. This was it, they were here for his soul.

Fear gripped the big man, and he was shaking all over. The tears began to fall as Squirrel wondered if he really had the courage to face this onslaught from the pits of hell. He had always talked a good game when it came to devil hunting, but this was the big show. He had always pictured a one on one battle with the devil, but he was greatly outnumbered here. Suddenly, a great resolve began to grow within him. Something seemed to click deep inside of him, and he felt a rage being born in his guts.

He looked all over the shack for a bible to beat back the horned devils with, but, sadly to say, Elmo and Melvin owned no bible. The doorbell kept ringing relentlessly. He could not stand it any longer. Hell was waiting outside, and it wasn't going away. Finally, he took off his leather belt, wrapped it a couple of turns around his fist, and charged outside into the night. He felt surrounded as he let out his best war cry, but he fought like a poet warrior.

He swung that belt with all his might, his war cry growing louder and louder each time the belt made contact with hell's minions. The devils seemed much smaller once he got outside amongst them. He was flogging them like his head was on fire and his ass was a-catchin'. The little devils were screaming out in horror and running to and fro. It was his finest hour. His mother would have been so proud of him.

When the battle was over, he stood exhausted and gasping for breath. He could hear devils still weeping and crying as they ran off into the night, no doubt headed back to hell to lick their wounds. The battlefield was his. As he looked around, he was absolutely amazed to see candy all over the ground. It was a true miracle. There were buckets of it just sitting there. It was God's reward for a job well done. The Lord had rewarded him and then some. Squirrel had never felt prouder of himself than he did at that moment. He gathered all the candy and went back inside the house. Within an hour, another band of devils stopped by the house. Squirrel whipped their asses too, and took their candy.

When Elmo and Melvin got home and opened the front door, Squirrel was stuffing candy bars in his mouth at a record pace. "You are not gonna believe what went down here tonight while you were gone, boys," said Squirrel, bouncing on some kind of sugar high from all the candy he had consumed. "I whipped the asses of no less than fourteen red devils this very night along with some lesser demons in the forms of wildlife and fairies. They were smaller than you might think, and God makes them carry candy around to give to whoever can whip their asses. I'm loaded down, boys, help yourselves!"

Before Elmo or Melvin could open their mouths, the doorbell rang again. "Watch this, boys," said Squirrel, yanking the door open. As he opened the door, an exceptionally large man, also in a devil costume, hit Squirrel right in the face. The big devil was the grandfather of one of Squirrel's earlier victims. The man then commenced beating the living hell out of Squirrel right there in Elmo's living room. Elmo and Melvin were not sure what to do, so they just watched. Finally, the big devil got tired and left Squirrel laying there in a pool of blood and candy.

CHAPTER 24

Elmo and Melvin cleaned Squirrel up and nursed his wounds the best they could. It took them the better part of an hour to convince him that the underworld had not descended upon the shack that night. Squirrel was disgusted to find that the outside world, which included everyone not from the hills, celebrated a holiday in which people dressed up like devils and begged for candy.

"I'm too tired and beat up to argue the point," said Squirrel, "but I am not totally convinced that those weren't real devils. I have experience with these matters, I have been on the devil's trail for years. Did you know he can shapeshift? Twice up in the hills, I was able to take a shot at him, but by the time I got there, he had already turned back into our neighbor's cow one time and our neighbor's horse the other time."

"Squirrel, you have got to stop with all this devil hunting," said Elmo. "We are trying to keep a family from being killed. You want some devils? Fine, I've got three for you that are about to burn up a mother and her children for money. I'm going to bed."

The next morning found everyone in a slightly better mood but nervous. The night Elmo and Melvin hid in Duffie's attic and heard the plans for the Sanders family, the three evil men had adjourned their little meeting by saying they would have one more meeting in exactly two weeks before the big event. The two weeks had gone by quickly. Besides signing up a crazy devil hunter on their team, Elmo and Melvin had accomplished very little over the last couple of weeks. The boys decided that Elmo would sneak back into Duffie's home that night and hide in the attic once again. They had to know if the Duffies' plan was still in motion and if any changes had been made to that plan. Melvin did not like the prospect of staying home alone with Squirrel, but he liked even less the prospect of being in Duffie's attic with three would-be killers in the house.

That evening, the three friends left while it was still daylight. Elmo knew what shift Duffie was working, so the meeting would probably take place about the same time the first one had. He wanted to get to the attic in plenty of time to overhear everything. Elmo had Squirrel and Melvin drop him off far from the Duffie house and told them to pick him up at the same spot at midnight. He then worked his way through some trees until he was in sight of the house.

Everything looked clear, so he made his way into the house and up into the attic. The house still stank terribly. The aging turds just would not let go of their grip on the residence. It was hot in the attic as he waited. His mind, as it had done so many times lately, seemed to be stuck on Rebecca Sanders. It was crazy to think that someone like her would have any interest in a loser like him. He had no prospects at all. He wasn't good looking, he wasn't smart, he wasn't a good person, and he certainly had no money. He didn't know how he was going to do it, but he knew that he had to save Rebecca and her family.

Squirrel and Melvin had decided to go get a big Slurpee at the bowling alley in Eltonberry. Squirrel was driving, and Melvin was afraid for his life. Squirrel took every curve at a high rate of speed. When they hit a raccoon crossing the road, Squirrel was devastated. He pulled the car over and began to weep. He insisted that Melvin get out of the car so they could say a few words over the dead coon.

"I will not. I don't care that it is dead. I'm even glad it's dead," insisted Melvin. "I'm tired of you selling crazy, I'm not buying anymore."

"You will help me with this service, or you will sit here until midnight on the side of this highway," said Squirrel, dangling the El Camino keys in Melvin's face.

Melvin wanted a cherry Slurpee bad, so he reluctantly went along. Squirrel picked a wildflower and laid it on the raccoon's belly, crossing his little arms over the flower. Squirrel then demanded they sing "Amazing Grace." The service concluded with Squirrel praying that the little coon would go to heaven and with Melvin quietly praying that Squirrel would die and go to hell.

When they finally rolled into Eltonberry, Squirrel slammed on the brakes as they were driving past the laundromat. "Oh, God give me strength!" screamed Squirrel. Squirrel jerked the El Camino into the parking lot, slammed on the brakes, and ran into the laundromat, screaming for Melvin to follow.

There was only one man in the laundromat. An overweight gentleman wearing a green leisure suit had his back to the door and was looking into the dryer as his clothes were almost done. The man had several gold caps on his teeth and had a slight limp from a recently sprained ankle. Squirrel charged the unaware man and pinned him up against the dryer. Squirrel began to feel and squeeze all over the man's backside in what appeared to be some strange, sexual attack. The man was screaming for help as Squirrel kept squeezing his behind. Finally, the man fell down to the floor, still screaming out for help. Squirrel grabbed one of his legs, ripped off his shoe and sock, and examined the man's heel as the guy fought and kicked. The last thing Squirrel did was feel all over the man's head. Suddenly, the attack stopped just as abruptly as it had begun.

"I do apologize for the inconvenience, guy, but I had to check for a rolled-up tail, cloven hooves, and for horns. This is an unfortunate case of mistaken identity. You perfectly fit the description of a devil given to me by a strange man in an elevator. I now believe he was less than truthful with me. Don't worry, I have experience in these matters. You have a good day now."

As Squirrel and Melvin ran back to the car, the man was weeping and shouting profanities. Melvin got behind the wheel and sped back to the shack in case the police would be in pursuit. He hated Squirrel with a passion. He had really wanted that cherry Slurpee.

CHAPTER 25

Every nerve in Elmo's body froze in time as he heard the front door open and the sounds of the three men talking as they came inside the house. True to their word, they had indeed shown up for their second meeting. Elmo figured he had already lost two pounds worth of sweat since he'd taken his place in the stinky attic. Peter Scott and the Duffie brothers wasted no time with small talk. Peter Scott, as usual, took control of the meeting right away.

"Jack, what is the status on the woman and kids?"

"Well, she still hates my guts, but the paperwork has been signed. She signed the marriage papers, and then I had her sign the life insurance stuff without her even realizing what it was. There is a problem though. I wouldn't let her have a phone in the house, but I found out she walked to the neighbor's house and called her sister a few states away. From what the neighbor tells me, he listened in on her call, and there wasn't a lot said. She just said she was in trouble and needed some help."

"Well, hell's bells, Jack, you really let a bad door be opened up for us there, didn't you?"

"Look, I did not think the sister was an option. They had nothing to do with each other for years. I guess I was wrong because the sister is worried, and she is coming down here the day after tomorrow."

"Damn, this is going to blow up in our faces," interjected Sheriff Duffie. "It's not too late to forget the whole thing and figure out another way to pay off the syndicate."

"No, my good sheriff, it is way too late," responded Peter. "My sources tell me the syndicate is already getting a hit squad together, because they don't believe we can come up with the amount we owe. They are going to make examples out of us very soon. I have also already got multiple palms greased up the insurance ladder, and the coroner is a dear friend of mine. Jack has the paperwork signed, we can still make this happen, but it has to happen tomorrow night before the sister shows up."

The three men argued, went back and forth, and eventually agreed that it would happen the next night at exactly midnight. Elmo wished he were one of those badass hero types in the movies that he and Melvin watched, but he was scared. Elmo was a rascal for sure, but he had never considered himself truly evil. These men were evil. They were going to kill this precious family in just a matter of twenty-four hours. They didn't have tails, cloven hooves, pitchforks, or red capes. They were just ordinary men who chose evil. Ordinary men that chose to be selfish to extreme limits. They would go home and kiss their own wives and children, make sure their loved ones were warm and safe, and do anything to protect their families. But Rebecca Sanders and her family just didn't matter enough to live.

"Jack, you better make damn sure that woman doesn't make any more phone calls," said Peter. "And she and the kids have got to be in that house at exactly midnight. You go stay over there tonight to make sure nothing gets in the way of this plan. I hate this as much as you two hate it, but after this is done, it will soon be a distant memory. We will never speak of it again, and our debts will also be a distant memory."

The three men went on to discuss more details on the setting of the fire and how distraught Jack would have to sound and act in the days after the fire. The men agreed that they owned the story at this point, and they needed everyone to understand how desperately Jack loved this woman and her kids. A lot of tears at the funeral would be a necessity. There was no way the professional they were going to use to set the fire could be there within twenty-four hours, so to make it fair to each of them, they agreed they would all three set the fire together.

Elmo looked down at his hands and noticed they were actually shaking. He was angry, and he was afraid. Elmo was truly overwhelmed. Elmo was just overwhelmed with the entire situation. He had never been an overly brave soul, but he knew he could not live with himself if he let the Sanders family down. After a while, Elmo heard the door shut. He snuck down and took a peek out of one of the windows. The three men were out by the sheriff's patrol car, smoking cigarettes. Elmo quietly snuck out the back door and worked his way through the darkness where Squirrel and Melvin were waiting to pick him up.

Elmo described in detail everything he had heard. Once back at the shack, it was time to piss or get off the porch. It was agreed that no one would go to bed until they had a plan in place to save the Sanders family.

"You know those three men will try and kill us if we attempt to intervene tomorrow night," said Elmo. "We've really only got two obvious choices that I can see. We can try to kill those three men, or we can try to go to the authorities in the morning."

"How can we kill anybody? We could not even kill the farmer's old, black dog, Elmo. We have adopted it for God's sake. And Squirrel, no offense to you, but I've seen nothing out of you to make me feel very secure in how savage you could be. I mean, my God, we had a funeral service for a dead raccoon this afternoon. I say we try to go to the authorities," said Melvin.

"If they have got connections all over the place, and we go to the wrong one, then the Sanders family will be dead for sure along with us. We would be gambling with their lives and our own. I've never wanted to kill anyone aside from devils, but I don't see any other way to save this poor family," said Squirrel, surprising the other two men by actually making sense.

"Here is where I'm at," said Elmo. "You two tell me if you have a better idea. We are not killers, but we are willing to do anything to save that family. Maybe killing these men is the only way, but I think there is another way. I believe we can trust Judge Clayton. He has always tried to be decent to us, Melvin. When I was in the attic, Peter Scott and the Duffie brothers agreed to meet at the sheriff's house at eleven o'clock tomorrow night and then head over to the Sanders' home together. What if we were able to sneak the Sanders out of their house at about eleven o'clock with Judge Clayton watching from the bushes. He would see that we were telling the truth as he watched those three scumbags torch the Sanders' home. He would then be able to help us with getting to someone high enough up the law enforcement food chain to deal with Sheriff Duffie and his buddies."

After a little more arguing and some more working out of details, it was voted on and agreed upon unanimously.

It was agreed that Elmo would go over and talk to the Sanders family and to Judge Clayton the next day, Squirrel would try to come up with some kind of weapons, and Melvin would map out a safe place to get the Sanders to, once rescued from the house. The three men all turned in and tried their best to get some sleep to no avail.

CHAPTER 26

Elmo woke up gasping for air and soaking wet. He thought Melvin had pissed in the bed for a second, but he realized quickly he was just covered in sweat. He had just had a terrible nightmare. In the nightmare, he had been sleeping peacefully in a room. In another room connected to his, Rebecca and her children were resting peacefully when a terrible fire broke out. He kept on sleeping in the dream even though the Sanders family was screaming as loud as they could for help. Elmo never could wake up during the dream, and the family died in the fire.

Elmo was very upset and went into the kitchen to get a glass of milk. Squirrel and Melvin were still sleeping. As Elmo sat down on the couch to drink his milk, the old, black dog came and sat in his lap. The dog slept in the bed with one of the boys every night since they adopted it. Since Squirrel had taken over Melvin's room, the dog slept between Elmo and Melvin. They could not remember life before the dog and could not imagine life without it. Elmo paced the house until he just couldn't do it anymore. Finally, he decided to go to Eltonberry's only all-night diner and get a cup of coffee. The dog jumped in the El Camino to go along for the ride.

He rolled the window down as he drove. It was a cool night, and the wind felt good on his face. Elmo could not help but wonder if it was the last night he would enjoy on this side of eternity. Everything looks different when faced with one's end. When he walked into the diner, Elder Johnson was sitting alone at a booth and nursing a cup of steaming hot coffee. To Elmo's surprise, he motioned for Elmo to come over and join him.

"Hello, Brother Elmo, what brings you out this time of night?"

"Oh, I couldn't sleep. It's a long story. I'm sorry again about setting your church on fire, Elder Johnson."

"Oh, that's all right, Elmo. I'm the one that should be sorry. I should not have slapped you across your face that day. I have regretted it ever since. Churches can be rebuilt, sometimes people can't. I had to go check on some of my church members that were involved in a little fender bender earlier tonight, so I thought a little coffee break might be in order."

Neither man spoke for a couple of minutes. The diner was almost empty. Somewhere back in the kitchen, a small radio was tuned in to an oldies station. One of the waitresses had on a perfume that smelled of lavender. The place had a peaceful feel to it that night.

"Elmo, I'm not one to stick my nose into other people's business, but you sure have a mighty heavy look to your countenance tonight. Is anything wrong?"

"Elder Johnson, have you ever been faced with something that was just too big for you to handle? I think

God must have got his files mixed up on me. I can't go into any details, but I am way out of my comfort zone with some stuff that has been thrown into my lap. God ought to do his homework a little better. Having people depending on me was a big mistake, I'm afraid."

"Elmo, I think it is you that has made the mistake. If God placed something in your lap, it was for a reason. He could have put it in mine or anyone else's, but he chose your lap to throw this situation into. I have a feeling that God believes in you a lot more than you believe in yourself. There are many things I feel inadequate to deal with as a pastor, husband, and a father, but sometimes we just have to take a stand and do the best we can. One of the keys to this life is to find something or someone worth fighting for, and then put up the best fight you can."

"But I'm afraid I can't win this fight, Elder Johnson," said Elmo.

"Elmo, it's okay to be afraid. Did you know that Jesus Christ was very afraid in the hours leading up to the Cross? The bible talks in detail about the terrible fear and anxiety he was facing. But Jesus decided that we, as his sinful children, were worth fighting for. So, he took all his fear, his anxiety, and our sins to the Cross of Calvary and died for us. He had found what was worth fighting for."

"I expect that's true, Elder. I'm just not a brave kind of guy."

"You don't have to be brave, Elmo. Remember, you don't have to win, you just have to fight. You'll find that if you're willing to fight for someone else, God will take care of a lot of the heavy lifting. The battle is ultimately the Lord's, but we have to play our part. I have got to get going, or Sister Johnson will call out the national guard to start looking for me. I want you to know that I'll be praying for you and your situation, whatever it is."

Elder Johnson said his goodbye, and left Elmo alone with his thoughts. It was a dangerous place to be lately. Looking out the diner's window, Elmo saw Elder Johnson stop by the El Camino and lean down with a big smile on his face. He saw him pet the old, black dog and say something before he disappeared into the night. When Elmo finished his coffee, he headed over in the general direction of the Sanders home. He drove near the end of their driveway and killed his engine. Rebecca's beat-up face had haunted his dreams since the first time he'd laid eyes on it. He'd only heard her voice for a moment the day he had stopped by, pretending to be house shopping, but he thought about it a lot.

He imagined Rebecca had probably had a rough go of things. Life seemed so kind to some and so ruthless to others. Without a doubt, many a tear had fallen in that house. There was a fog out that night, but even through the fog, the darkness surrounding the Sanders' home seemed almost alive. A darkness older than the very earth it covered. Elmo had always thought of the darkness as just part of a natural world too big to understand. It had never occurred to him that perhaps there was more to the darkness than he thought. What if that darkness knew exactly what it was doing? What if it had an agenda? What if it was a living thing that fed on the innocent, the helpless, and the weak?

The Sanders family was not unique, though. They were just another meal for something that had eaten countless families for ages untold. Elmo swallowed hard and felt the dryness in his throat. He wished it had been someone else in Sheriff Duffie's attic that night, but it was him. Tomorrow night Elmo Bogg knew, for the first time in his life, he would challenge that darkness. The sun was starting to rise, so Elmo started his car and headed back home to awaken his sleeping army.

CHAPTER 27

E lmo made his two soldiers a hearty breakfast. Bacon, eggs, grits, and drop biscuits would fuel them through what was to come. The trio didn't voice it, but they were each hoping that it would not be their last meal. As Elmo watched the two men eat their food, he had a good feeling wash over him. He had always heard it said that a man could count his true friends on one hand and have fingers left over. Elmo knew he only needed two of the fingers on that one hand, but, oh, what splendid fingers they were. They were misfits to society, perhaps, but they were true friends to ride the river with.

"Here is the plan, boys. I'm going over to Judge Clayton's house about nine this morning to try and talk him into coming tonight. Melvin, you go gas up the El Camino. Squirrel, I want you to find us some weapons for tonight. If you have to, just go out into the woods, and find us some big, thick limbs. There's a saw out in the tool shed if you need to do any cutting."

"I thought we were going to try and do this with no fighting," protested Melvin.

"That is the plan, Melvin, but we should be ready in case things don't go the way we planned. Just relax, everything is going to be all right," said Elmo, hoping he sounded more confident than he actually was.

When Elmo got to Judge Clayton's house, his stomach was in knots. He wasn't sure if it was because of the coming showdown, or if it was because he knew the terrible Bull Clayton was behind the door he was about to knock on. Bull's new nurse answered the door. She looked mean enough to melt butter, and Elmo knew, from experience, that was exactly the kind of nurse Bull needed and deserved.

"Is Judge Clayton here?" asked Elmo.

"No, he is not," snapped the nurse. "What do you need?"

"My name is Elmo Bogg, and I need to talk to him pretty bad. Do you know when he will be back?"

"He will be out of town for the next three days, and I have no way to get ahold of him. Good day," said the woman as she slammed the door in Elmo's face.

Elmo was devastated. All his carefully laid plans were useless if Judge Clayton was out of town. Halfway back to the car, a crazy thought struck Elmo. He stopped in his tracks and headed back to the Clayton home. Instead of going back to the front door, he went to the side of the house where Bull's room was. He gently knocked on the window, hoping Nurse Ratchet didn't hear. He was about to leave when the window opened, and a very strong and aged hand grabbed him by the throat. The other hand was holding a knife.

"Well, what do we have here? Did you come back for some sweet revenge, boy?"

"Let me go, Bull, I can't breathe," gasped Elmo.

Bull relaxed his grip a little, and Elmo got right to the point. "Bull, I know this sounds crazy, but I need your help. You are the single meanest human being I have ever met, and I could sure use some of that meanness on my side tonight. I'm in big trouble."

Elmo spent the next thirty minutes laying out the entire story for Bull Clayton. Bull was not overly receptive until he heard the part about three innocent children being burned up for money. Hearing that he would be going to war against a crooked law man was right up his alley too. Mostly Bull Clayton just wanted one more adventure, and the truth was he actually kind of liked Elmo a little. Bull signed up and agreed to call his partner in crime, Leroy, who had helped paint Elmo into a rainbow with the paint guns.

"In case you haven't noticed, boy, we're old farts. We don't get around too good or too fast, but I believe we could be of some help to those three little children tonight."

Elmo went over what had been the plan with Bull. "I guess we will have to figure something else out now, since Judge Clayton is out of town."

"You don't need my son and the law tonight. Nurse Jackass was not lying. My son will be very difficult to reach for the next couple of days, but I will try and make a few calls. My guess is he will not get my message until far too late, so you and I are going to make a new plan right now. Leroy and I will be there. We will save that little family, or we will all die together trying to save them. You and your little queer friends just make sure you all are there when it's go time."

Elmo and Bull shook on it, and his little army was starting to grow. He was feeling just a little better and not quite as alone. Bull and Leroy might be old, but they were meaner than snakes and twice as tricky. It would still be Elmo's job to get Rebecca and her family out of the house before the three villains got there. Elmo got in the car and headed for Rebecca's house, but Jack's car was there. For four hours, Elmo drove back and forth past the Sanders' home and observed it from the highway, but Jack's car never left.

It dawned on Elmo that Jack wasn't about to take a chance on Rebecca leaving or making any more phone calls. Jack and the others had to kill the Sanders family tonight before that sister got into town tomorrow. Jack was not going to leave the Sanders' place until he met his other two conspirators at Sheriff Duffie's house at eleven o'clock, just like they had planned on. It might be better this way after all. Rebecca would not have the fear and anxiety all day long of knowing what was coming later that night. As soon as Jack left for the eleven o'clock meeting at the Sheriff's house, Elmo would be in the shadows ready to get the family informed and out of the house as fast as possible. The sun was starting to go down. It was time to get back to the boys and put their plan into motion.

Elder Johnson had said to find someone or something worth fighting for, and then get to fighting. Elmo took one more look at the little house, and he understood very clearly what the old gentleman had meant.

CHAPTER 28

When Elmo got back to the shack that afternoon, only Melvin and their dog were there. "Where is Squirrel at?" asked Elmo.

"He said he had to go get his secret weapon," responded Melvin.

"What the heck does that mean?"

Before Melvin could even respond, the door burst open and Squirrel walked in followed by Big Sue. She had on her brass knuckles and looked ready to hurt anyone who got too close. "What's going on, Squirrel? What is Big Sue doing here?"

"Now is as good a time as any to announce that we have started dating," said Squirrel. "My battles are hers, and her battles are mine. Also, her name is not Big Sue, it is just Sue, if you please. We need all the help we can get tonight, don't you think?"

It did not take Elmo long to get on board as he looked at the brass knuckles on Sue's hand and the ever-present snarl on her face. "I sure do agree, and welcome aboard Sue. I am delighted to have you on our team." Elmo filled everyone in on the fact that Bull and Leroy were now on their team also, and would be there for the battle. The Sanders home was surrounded by forest and in an isolated area. The Bogg team agreed to take positions all around the Sanders home at the edge of the tree line as darkness fell, and to attack from every direction at the pivotal moment. Squirrel had multiple oak limbs he had gathered and prepared for the battle. At eight o'clock, Bull Clayton called the shack to confirm that he had not heard back from his son that day. The battle had to take place after all. They all squeezed into the El Camino and headed for the Sanders family. They parked far from the home on a logging road inside the cover of the forest, and after wishing each other luck, they made their way through the forest at different angles and took up positions just inside the tree line and around the house. There was no sign of Bull and Leroy, but that could be a good sign, thought Elmo. Bull could have gotten ahold of Judge Clayton, and the real cavalry could be headed this way. But Elmo knew he had to approach things as if the battle was theirs alone. Sue had her brass knuckles, Elmo and Squirrel had their oak limbs, and Melvin had an old aluminum baseball bat that Squirrel had "borrowed" from a yard in Eltonberry.

The first fly in the ointment came when, at eleven o'clock, Jack Duffie did not get in his vehicle and leave. The Duffies' plan had obviously changed some. Jack was apparently at the house to make sure nothing went wrong, and Peter Scott and the Sheriff would be coming to join him on site. This made their evacuation plan of Rebecca and the kids impossible. At ten minutes after eleven, Jack Duffie quietly eased the door open and stepped outside.

He lit a cigarette and walked to the edge of the driveway without ever making a sound.

Rebecca had taken to locking herself and her kids in her room each night that Jack stayed over in case he ever got any ideas during the night. She must have heard the door creak a little or something, because something had awakened her from sleep. She quietly opened the door and eased outside to the porch swing. She did not realize that Jack had left the house already ahead of her. The night was cool, and Rebecca had her afghan wrapped tight around her. As she swung slowly in the swing, she began to hum an old tune she remembered from her childhood. Elmo was still in the shadows, watching the driveway through the moonlight. And then he saw what he had been dreading. Three dark figures walked silently up the driveway closer and closer to Rebecca's house. The only sound in the dark, sacred night was the humming of an old Irish tune and the beating of many nervous hearts.

Peter Scott was pissed off. People could be so inconsiderate. Why couldn't this woman and her kids just be asleep, so his job would be easier? Rebecca being awake would make it messier, but it was still going to get done. She could scream, but no one lived close enough to hear her. Jack had made sure she owned no cell phone and had no landline either. Jack stepped forward and called out her name. Rebecca gasped and jumped up from the swing.

"There is nowhere to run to, Rebecca. Just stay calm and don't wake up the kids. This will all be over soon."

"Jack, is that you? Who else is with you, and what do you want?" asked Rebecca, her voice cracking just a little.

"It's not a matter of what we want, it is more a matter of what we need. We need the insurance money from you and those kids. We hate to do it, but there is going to be a fire inside your home tonight, Rebecca," said Jack Duffie.

Rebecca grabbed the only thing within reach, an old broom, and took a defensive position before her front door. She felt a terror inside of her that she had never known before as the impact of Jack's words hit home. She had known for some time that Jack was an evil man, but she had grossly underestimated just how evil. The three men started for the house and Rebecca.

Elmo looked down and saw his hands trembling terribly. He wanted to move, but his body felt almost frozen. He felt ashamed that he was so scared. Rebecca's face was illuminated just a little bit by the moonlight. Elmo could see the fear and desperation of a woman that had no more outs. Elmo knew at that moment, for the first time in a long time, he was about to really and truly do the right thing. As he stared at Rebecca, Elmo Bogg knew he could stop looking for his treasure. He had already found it. He would save her or die with her, but he would stand in the shadows no longer. For the first time in his life, Elmo Bogg stepped forth out of the shadows.

"That's close enough, boys," said Elmo, the oak limb hanging at his side.

The Duffies and Peter Scott spun in his direction in absolute shock. "Who's there?" shouted Sheriff Duffie.

"This is Elmo Bogg, and I know what you came here to do tonight. It's not going to happen, you fat pig."

"Bogg, you little bastard, I don't know how you're here, but I'm glad you are here. Now we have a perfect patsy to take the blame after we torch your girlfriend and her little ones. We arrived on the scene not long after you set fire to the house. We tried to get the Sanders family out, but the flames overwhelmed us. And finally, you went for my gun, and I had to shoot you through your freakin' heart."

"This is excellent, Duffie," said Peter Scott. "This could not have worked out better."

"That is true, Peter, but first I'm going to beat his little ass. I've hated him for a long time," growled Sheriff Duffie.

Duffie had been rolling his sleeves up as he talked. He handed his gun belt over to Jack and charged Elmo at a dead run. Duffie had not noticed the oak limb dangling from Elmo's hand in the darkness. As he was almost on top of Elmo, Elmo swung the limb as hard as he could right at Duffie's torso. The thud was unmistakable as oak met gut. Duffie collapsed in a heap on the ground, gasping for air. Elmo followed that up with a whack to the Sheriff's head.

Elmo then charged Jack and Peter, but he tripped on a tricycle laying in the yard that he did not see. Jack Duffie and Peter Scott went to work on Elmo, kicking him over and over. Elmo struggled back up to his feet and swung a right hook that caught Jack on the nose, sending him to the ground. He landed a good knee into Peter Scott's privy area, but Sheriff Duffie had regained his composure and rejoined the fight. Elmo was doing his best, but he could not handle the three bigger men. After the men had quickly beat him to a pulp, Elmo lay on the ground, bleeding. He felt as though he were on the verge of blacking out.

The men walked past Elmo's body, and he could hear them grab Rebecca and slap her a ringing blow across the face. Peter Scott hit Rebecca in the stomach. She doubled over on the ground. Sheriff Duffie grabbed her by the hair and was about to drag her back into the house. Duffie looked up just in time to see Squirrel charging him with a huge oak limb. His face was painted blue and white, and he was screaming his war whoop as he ran. The sheriff tried to jump out of the way, but it was too late. Squirrel hit him directly across the forehead, and Duffie went down like a ton of bricks. Sue had taken those brass knuckles and commenced beating the living hell out of Jack Duffie. He did not stand a chance against the determined Sue.

Peter Scott was not in the mood for any more fighting. They had a fire to start. Peter had picked up Sheriff Duffie's gun off the ground where it had fallen. Just as Elmo stood back up to get back in the fight, Scott squeezed off a shot. The bullet grazed Elmo's shoulder, sending him sprawling to the ground. His arm felt warm and wet. Peter was now standing over Elmo and pointing the gun right at Elmo's head. Elmo knew he was about to die. Death is never real until the very moment it taps you on the shoulder.

Suddenly, there was a growling sound coming from somewhere in the darkness. Peter looked up just as something flew out of the bushes and bit into his leg. Peter let out a scream and took a shot at his attacker. Elmo looked up in time to see the old, black dog they thought they had left at home. Peter fired again, and this time the bullet found its mark to some degree. The dog cried out and limped back into the darkness. Little did he know that dog could not be killed, thought Elmo. Melvin had now joined the battle and put that aluminum bat right across Peter Scott's head. The entire battle thus far had lasted for only a couple of minutes, but Sheriff Duffie and his brother had just got back up on their feet when things changed without warning.

The sound of horse's hooves came charging out of the darkness. Bull Clayton and Leroy were swinging lariat ropes as they charged the Duffie brothers. The brothers ran, but to no avail. The old men lassoed the two brothers, wrapped the rope around the saddle horns, and dragged the Duffie brothers into the darkness of the forest at full speed. Peter Scott was laying on the ground and not moving. His eyes were glazed over in death. Melvin's swing of the bat seemed to have done him in. From somewhere in the forest, two gunshots rang out and shattered the silence of the night. In just a little while, Bull and Leroy came galloping back on their horses with no Duffies in tow.

Squirrel and Melvin ran over to Elmo, trying to see how badly his shoulder was hurt. Elmo's shoulder was bleeding, but the bullet had only grazed him. The three friends froze when they heard the unmistakable sound of a revolver cocking. Peter Scott had gotten back up and had the sheriff's gun in his outstretched hand, pointing it at the boys. There was blood flowing from his forehead and hate in his eyes. Suddenly, there was a tap on Peter Scott's shoulder from behind. As he turned around to see who it was, he was just in time to see Sue and her brass knuckles closing in on his chin. Peter Scott went down and was out cold this time. Just as quickly as it had started, the entire battle was over.

After everyone had caught their breath, Elmo and his entire army embraced and began to cry, they were so happy. The terrible ordeal was over, and they had done it. Rebecca Sanders and her children were safe. Rebecca was still on the ground. She had been hit a hard blow across the face, which had opened up a nasty cut above her eye. Elmo gently helped her to her feet. She was weak and leaned against Elmo for support. Elmo didn't say anything. He just put a gentle arm around her and hugged a woman that desperately needed to be hugged.

Bull Clayton had taken charge. Leroy had already tied another rope around Peter Scott and had dragged him into the forest down the same path the Duffies had been dragged down. It was the same path all evil eventually gets dragged down. "Listen to me well, everyone," said Bull. "This night never happened. It never took place. No matter who might ask you or for what reason they might ask you, this night never took place. We were never here. Miss Sanders, when you are questioned about the disappearance of Jack Duffie, he was gone when you woke up from a full night's sleep. These men will never be seen or heard from again, but I want solid commitments of silence from all around. I don't ever want to be asked any questions about what happened to these men, not even from you all. Leroy and I will take it from here. We have experience in such matters, and it is the only way to keep this family safe going forward. These men could never have allowed the Sanders family to live if they walked away from this."

Everyone agreed to a pact of silence. Without any more talk, Bull rode off on his horse to join Leroy. They all sat on the front porch, and they filled Rebecca in on all that had happened since that first night Elmo and Melvin had been in the sheriff's attic. Not long after, a nice truck and horse trailer came pulling out of the forest on one of the old logging roads and was soon heading down Rebecca's driveway for the main road. As Elmo watched the two old veterans disappear into the night, he was quite sure there was more than horses in the back of that trailer.

The war party was invited inside the house, as no one would be able to sleep that night anyway. As morning dawned, Rebecca made them all some breakfast. Three little faces joined them for breakfast. They especially liked Sue and were combing her hair in no time. Sue never growled once and even smiled a few times. The smile looked good on her.

Bull was true to his word. Sheriff John Duffie, Jack Duffie, and Peter Scott were never seen or heard from again. A massive search lasted for three weeks, but not a single hair was ever found of the three men. It was rumored they fell into the hands of loan sharks over a gambling debt.

CHAPTER 29

Two weeks after that fateful night at the Sanders home, Elmo, Melvin, and Squirrel were dressed to the hilt. Squirrel had even splurged on brand new underwear. There would be no holes this night. They were getting ready for a barbeque at Rebecca Sanders' house. Elmo had already been on two dates with Rebecca, one of them without Melvin.

Squirrel had finally romanced Sue enough to get through to the softer stuff on the inside. They had been on five dates already. Sue had quit growling at folks altogether, and she rarely hit anyone in the face anymore. Melvin was not dating, but he was looking forward to the barbeque all the same. Rebecca's sister had decided to stay down for a while to look after Rebecca and the kids, and Melvin was a little sweet on big sister.

Elmo had gone back to work for Judge Clayton watching Bull six days a week. The arrangement had come at Bull's request, and the two were becoming real friends. Elmo still had to be careful, understanding full well that people as dangerous as Bull could never be handled casually. Tigers did not change their stripes, and no matter how much one wanted a tiger to be a bunny rabbit, it was still a tiger. But things were much better, and the two were starting to really enjoy each other's company.

As the El Camino pulled up in the Sanders' yard, Bull and Leroy were already on the porch telling stories to Rebecca's three children. Sue was tending the barbeque pit, and she had a smile on her face as Squirrel got out of the car. Elmo gave Rebecca a big hug and even a peck on the cheek. Soon, a heated game of horseshoes was going on between Squirrel and Melvin. Squirrel tried to enforce rules from the hills, which seemed to contradict the rest of the world's rules. Bull and Leroy had brought their paint guns and were teaching the Sanders children to be excellent little marksmen. Elmo was delighted to see Elder Johnson pulling up. He had accepted Elmo's invitation.

"I never refuse the offers of good food, good fellowship, and good friends," said Elder Johnson.

Soon, Squirrel was talking Elder Johnson's ears off about his many adventures while chasing devils up in the hills. Elmo found a few minutes while everyone was doing something, and he slipped off behind Rebecca's house. For the first time in his life, Elmo bowed his head, and he said a real prayer. He was not sure what to say, so he just reached down deep inside and said the one thing he felt the most in his life lately. He said, "thank you," and promised more to come at a more private moment.

Rebecca slipped up behind him and put a soft hand on his back. Elmo did not say a word. He just took her in his arms and kissed her. He kissed her like she was a lost treasure recently found. There was a little hill not too far away that overlooked the Sanders home. Up on the top of that hill, the old, black dog that saved Elmo's life was laying down and watching the festivities.

The old dog watched people that had been knocked down over and over and over for their entire lives. The dog watched people that somehow had always managed to get back up just one more time, always one more time. The dog saw them smiling, laughing, and celebrating life. Through the bruises, blood, and tears that life had brought them, they smiled. With enough abuse and heartache in their rearview mirrors to fill an entire library, they laughed. Without two cents to rub together and no control over their tomorrow, they celebrated life. The faint smell of barbeque made its way up the little hill. Squirrel surprised them all by pulling out a fiddle and playing them a lively tune from the hill country. The old, black dog seemed to almost smile as the people below began to dance around the yard. The old dog put her head down and died in peace.

A NOTE FROM THE AUTHOR

Thank you for reading Elmo Bogg. I hope there are some lessons we can take from Elmo and Melvin. No one got their backside beat down and beat up as much as Elmo Bogg, but he always managed to stand back up one more time. Some of you have been broken into too many pieces to count, but it is not time to give up. Some of you have been abused and used in terrible ways. You should never have had to endure that, but it is not time to give up. Some of you are damaged, hurt, and at the end of your rope, but it is not time to give up. Some of you are addicted and feel very alone right now, but it is not time to give up. Some of you have considered checking out of this game early because of all the heartache and pain, but it is not time to give up. Some of you are sick and hurting, but don't give up yet. It is dark right now, but daylight is on the way. Jesus Christ loves you more than you can possibly understand. He is closer than you know. If you think you are too dirty for Him or you've messed up too much for His help, you have no idea who He really is. He is an expert at cleaning up messes, and He is after your heart. You don't have to understand Him to trust Him. His Blood and Holy Spirit will make all the difference in the world for you and your family. He doesn't make all our problems go away, that is for sure. But we do not have to ever go through our problems alone again. You don't have to understand, but He is closer than you know. You might even have to forgive Him for some things that don't make sense to you from your past, but it will be worth it. I give you my word that He has not forgotten you. Wipe off the dirt, blood, and dust and stand yourself back up one more time, just like Elmo. Always one more time. You will never be perfect, but you can be redeemed. You can handle this fight, and you are not alone. With all the pain and heartache, this life is still worth it. Life is always worth it.

Made in the USA
Columbia, SC
04 February 2021

32229765R00088